REALM OF LOST SOULS

CHRONICLES OF THE SUPERNATURAL
BOOK TWO

J M HART

COPYRIGHT

INTRODUCTION

CHRONICLES OF THE SUPERNATURAL BOOK ONE: THE
EMERALD TABLET

When a team of archaeologists discover an unmarked tomb, all hell breaks loose. Unwittingly, they find and remove a lost artifact from Greek and Egyptian mythology which, for thousands of years, had sealed the gate to the dimension of Hell. Thought to have been owned by Hermes, 'Thrice Great,' and Thoth, the artifact, the Emerald Tablet, bestows upon its carrier the ability to open doorways into other dimensions and harness the wisdom of the entire universe; alchemy, astrology and the divine influence of humanity.

Desperate to heal his dying wife, one archaeologist, William O'Grady steals the artifact, accidentally killing his colleagues and his son's friend Rachel. He sells it to the highest bidder, a Russian oil tycoon living in Egypt, to pay for his wife's experimental treatment. The Russian promises O'Grady that if the cure is unsuccessful, he will allow him to make use of the powers of the artifact to take her into a dimensional space that will heal all her ailments. He lies, he refuses to loan the artifact, and O'Grady's wife dies a few months later.

Once the artifact is removed, viral shape-shifting demonic scavengers from Hell are released to roam the Earth, feeding on the negative thoughts of humankind and capturing their souls. However, the artifact doesn't perform for its new Russian owner. Shaun, the son of the archaeologist and one of the seven gifted teenagers, not understanding their importance, keep a pouch of gemstones originally from the tomb that are needed to activate the Emerald Tablet.

Ten years pass, and the same demonic scavengers become an invisible dominating species. The swarm has now reached the four corners of the Earth, searching for and possessing the selfish and attaching themselves to kindred energies. Men, woman and children become embodiments of rage and violence. The virus possesses the weak and self-loathing, then uses them all as puppets. It infiltrates first the lungs and brain, then the soul, and with one malevolent cough it spreads to the next unsuspecting weak soul, and the next. Hell's scavengers have one goal in mind—to destroy God's precious world.

Pockets of good people still exist scattered throughout the world like the seven young strangers, on different sides of the globe, Shaun, Kevin, Jade, Casey, Sophia, Tim, and Rachel. These seven individuals face their own personal traumas. They have gifts that will unfold and each has a piece of the puzzle that can help return the Emerald Tablet to its rightful place which will bring an end to the chaos and suffering. They must overcome the distance between each other physically and emotionally, but air and sea travel is prohibited; boarders are closed and just about every country is under martial law.

PROLOGUE

Tightly wrapped in sheets and doused in gasoline, the remaining fifteen bodies from the surrounding properties burned. Reverently, the small community of nineteen watched on. The Emerald Tablet had been returned and the gate to the underworld closed, but it was too early to tell if the prior damage was rectified.

Jade took another step back from the heat of the pyre to stand behind Kevin, the portal creator. He stood five feet eight inches tall, broad-shouldered, with a narrow waist, his hair golden brown. He was standing next to his best friend Tim. She wrapped her arms around Kevin and dug her hands into the pockets of his jacket. She knew he kept his bowie knife strapped to his side, as they all did. It was his sixteenth birthday on May 4th ... in one month. Jade had her sixteenth birthday in January. Casey and Shaun were both

Scorpios and had celebrated their birthdays together on Casey's fifteenth. Shaun had only mentioned his eighteenth birthday had come and gone because Casey had asked.

Despite the age differences, Shaun and Casey had become close friends, like Jade and Rachel. Rachel was the eldest—she had turned twenty in March, two days prior to Sophia's fifteenth—but she was the shortest. Even though Sophia was the youngest, she was considered the leader of the group and the most powerful.

Jade looked along the row of her new extraordinary friends. After the ordeals of the last seven months they had become family, but she knew it was time for them to separate. There was more to be done. The whiteout had blinded them to the world beyond for four weeks, and five months later, the sounds and shadows of the creatures that had lurked in the whiteout still caused Jade to think the world had changed. It was not the same world as the one before the return of the Emerald Tablet and the cleansing of the virus, and she had to admit she could feel it.

She was not the same. None of them were.

1

Jade left the herbs from her hydroponic garden on the kitchen table for Joe. Lucy was on guard, sleeping, and Jade patted her on the head. "I know how you feel, girl. I feel like a bear who forgot to hibernate for the winter." The sandy-colored Labrador wagged her tail but didn't bother getting up.

Deep in thought, Jade opened the door to the basement where everyone – *except our parents, or the dead*, as Tim would say – were welcome to gravitate to. Halfway down the stairs, she tripped. She reached for the banister to stop herself from falling, but couldn't quite get a grip and tumbled down the steps. Jade felt like she was falling in slow motion, and imagined the look on everyone's faces. She banged her head on the last step. Her skin prickled and the hairs on her arms rose as she passed through the static energy of the barrier

Sophia had created to keep the spirits of the dead from harassing Casey. *It must be difficult for Casey,* she thought. It was something she hoped she never had to experience.

Kevin and Casey jumped up from the settee to help her, and she felt a zap of energy at Kevin's touch.

"I'm okay," she told them. "What happened?"

"Oh, just bad lighting." *How embarrassing,* she thought. Once she found her father, the nightmares should stop, and then she wouldn't be stumbling around half asleep.

"It's the same lighting as always," said Shaun. "You need to get out of your own head, intel."

"I just haven't been sleeping well," said Jade. "Why?" asked Shaun.

She could feel Sophia's eyes on her, waiting for an answer.

"You done with my gemstones?" asked Shaun, when Jade didn't reply.

"Why don't you create a portal?" Rachel said to Kevin. She was sitting on an old trunk, with her legs crossed, eating strawberries fresh from their hydroponic garden.

Kevin sat down, swung his legs over the side of the settee and lay his head on Jade's leg. She combed her fingernails through his soft brown hair before placing a couple of cushions under his head. Jade picked up her notebook and Shaun's soft leather pouch containing his nine semi-precious gemstones. She opened the notebook, flicking through pages of drawings and notes on the herbs she had started growing. Jade flicked past sketches of Sophia blasting cars off the road with colored energy blasts; past images and details of Casey with his arms in the air, lifting the fuselage of the Cherokee off the front lawn with his mind, and Kevin standing in front of a shimmering portal he'd created, until she reached the last sketch, a finished drawing of Shaun's sacred geometric-shaped gemstones. Jade was meticulous about the gems and had drawn them using a ruler, a compass and a protractor she picked up during one of the supply runs into town.

Jade closed her eyes, twirling the gemstone between her fingers. She opened up her psyche, and listened to the stone, waiting for a message like Sophia had taught her. A thought was forming.It felt like a stifled scream trapped inside her body, then images and feelings erupted into her mind: the power of a nuclear reactor; overwhelming emotion, followed by stability, clarity and flow. She opened her eyes, and below the heading, Insights, Jade jotted down the details. She put the gemstone back inside Shaun's pouch and took out the Merkaba clear quartz and started sketching.

"Well," said Rachel as she repeated her question, "why *don't* you open a portal?"

Jade had her theories as to why Kevin wouldn't open a portal, but she didn't want to voice them. She had learned that it was best to let the others find answers, rather than offer her knowledge or opinion all the time. She was also afraid she would hurt Kevin's feelings since she had watched his sadness come and go over the past few months. He was angry at God and said it should have been him and not Alex; he felt guilty for being alive. Everyone's spirits had lifted when the twins were born two months ago, including Kevin's, but now, he just lacked motivation.

"If you like, K, I can unblock you," said Casey.

"Me too," said Sophia, "but you have to do the work yourself." "Okay, Buddha," Shaun said to Sophia. "Give him space. The guy lost his brother."

Kevin brushed his fringe back over his face and folded his arms across his chest.

"I need to find my family," said Rachel, "can't you just try?" "I'm afraid!" Kevin blurted out.

"Of what?" Shaun asked. "You were with me when we found the decomposing bodies, and not once did you shy away, or complain. You kept it together, man. You're strong and capable." Looking around the basement Shaun caught Rachel's eye, she was eating strawberries and tossed one to him. "Alex would be proud of his big brother. We all are. What are you afraid of K?"

Shaun never ceased to amaze Jade. When they had first met he was such an arrogant, thoughtless asshole. But Alex had changed him, and now Shaun cared for Kevin and Casey like a big brother. But not so much for Tim who, for some reason, got on Shaun's nerves. Yet it was Tim who had saved Rachel's life.

"What if I open a portal and we can't get back? What if I open a portal and someone else dies? What if I open a portal and find the whole world is dead?"

"We're all worried," said Sophia. "One day we will die. I looked into the future and saw only the whiteout. My dreams are empty and I've never known my dreams to be empty. That's why I focus on building the energy, creating stronger and stronger bursts of energy to blow shit up, like the cars and trucks that were used as roadblocks. I know people will come, but I haven't foreseen anything else and that scares me."

"We're all frightened," Jade said, finishing her sketch of the Merkaba clear quartz. She put the stone back in the pouch and tossed it to Shaun. "I'm concerned for my dad. I would like to go find him, when you're ready." Jade put her protractor, book and pencil on the side table.

Kevin sat up, rubbed the stubble on his face and cursed. He was going to do it. Jade could see it. He was angry, but he was going to open a portal. He stood and held his hands out to fold the space in front of him, which moved like liquid mercury; sparks of energy lit up the space between his hands. They heard the crackling, and a low hum filled the room. He stretched his arms wide. The familiar sound of a portal opening was exciting. Everyone was on their feet when Kevin stepped in. He disappeared and the portal quickly closed behind him. Seconds later, he opened the door at the top of the basement stairs. His features were hidden by the bright light from the kitchen.

"Tomorrow, Rachel, I'll open a portal for you to find your brother and mother. I'll give you one week. If you're not at the portal waiting for me when I return, I'll come for you."

"Jade, you're next. Go tell your mom we leave tomorrow

to find your dad." He slammed the door closed, leaving them looking at each other, dumbfounded.

"I told you he could do it," Tim said to Shaun. "He just needed you guys to push him."

Shaun high-fived Casey.

Rachel threw Sophia a strawberry. "They're really good."

Rachel tried not to sound too excited. Her lips were pressed tight, highlighting her natural dimples, which revealed the hidden smile. She picked up her long brown boots, slipped her bare feet in, and zipped them up along the inside of her lower legs. She was curvy with a narrow waist and full breasts. And she was mad for Shaun. Tim and Rachel had a special bond which Shaun didn't like, but accepted. Rachel treated Tim the same way she probably treated her younger brother.

Tomorrow, Jade was going to search for her dad and for some reason she felt it wasn't going to be easy. She took her notebook and went to tell her mom the good news. She would be ecstatic.

JADE COULD SEE SOPHIA, CROSS-LEGGED ON THE GRASS BY THE plane wreckage: she was checking the protective cloak around the estate. It was one of the first things Sophia did every morning. Tim called the shield a psychic condom. The sound of a car in the distance was notable, even before Jade could see it. A blue sedan approached, stopping by the front gate. A man, wearing a green parka, and a woman, stepped from the car. The woman reached into the back seat, grabbing a brown over-coat. They walked to the edge of the road, stopped and gazed in her direction – it was as if they sensed the presence of something beyond their field of vision. Jade counted how long it would take for them to give up searching for the unseen.

Four minutes, and they were climbing back into their car heading toward a ghost town. It was like the estate didn't exist. Nobody stopped for long. The longest had been a young man driving a beat-up red car. He hung around for twenty-seven minutes. Before leaving, he climbed onto the car roof and cried out. Jade had wanted to race down to the gate and let him in, but she wouldn't dare put the others in jeopardy. Sophia had said when someone can see through the protection, they will be able to join them.

An impression of her father struggling with demons popped into her mind, snapping her out of her trance. The images had been plaguing her psyche for nearly a month, and they were getting stronger. At first, the visions were only in her dreams. Many nights over the past couple of weeks, Jade had lain awake, afraid to sleep. She dug her nail into the knuckle on her index finger now, waiting for the image to go away.

She had become so tired; during the day she would fake cramps, just to be left alone to sleep. And when she couldn't sleep, she watched Casey and Sophia through the bedroom window, practicing their particular skills; sometimes Jade felt so inadequate she had to will herself to force the debilitating thoughts aside. She didn't think anyone knew she was watching, until one day Casey had raised Sophia and Tim off the ground. They had floated past her window and waved. Straightaway, she had heard the sound of someone charging up the stairs. She had expected Kevin to burst into the room, so when Rachel barged in muttering in Hebrew, she was surprised. Rachel had taken her hand and marched her downstairs, and Jade was glad she had. Jade joined in, and Casey lifted all of them off the ground together. Before they all fell down laughing, it had been a magical few seconds. He went on to raise only one or two of them at a time, in case he lost control. It was the most fantastic experience of freedom Jade had ever felt. Casey never levitated, never left the ground himself – Jade believed he was scared of heights. She looked up from her reverie to see Sophia watching her. Jade hadn't told anyone about the dreams and visions, but it was as if Sophia could sense her discomfort.

Two hours ago, Shaun and Rachel had left for Israel to find her brother and mother. Shaun buried his favorite gemstone in Alex's grave for safekeeping. It was now her turn to go home to South Carolina to bring her dad back to the estate. She was apprehensive, maybe a little frightened. With every tick of the clock, she felt more ill-at-ease.

It was no use, she was too nervous. Agitated, she pushed her hair back and tied it into a loose ponytail. Jade pulled her beanie off her head and cupped her hot face. She tilted her head back, welcoming the chilly wind and tried to focus on the wind passing through the trees, imagining soft snowflakes falling on her face—even though it was the middle of spring—it was still cold enough, but it hadn't snowed in weeks. Her body temperature dropped and her breathing relaxed. She twirled the silky ends of her hair and brushed them soothingly against her face. Her legs felt as if they had the onset of pins and needles. Jade shook her legs, trying to get the blood circulating. One minute she was on fire, the next her blood felt icy cold.

She pulled her puffer jacket tight and hugged herself as it suddenly started to snow. She looked up at the sky, blinking away the flakes, wondering why she was so edgy. Jade felt along her thigh for her bowie knife and checked it was secured to her leg. She didn't think she would need it, but she liked the feeling it gave her, and it wasn't just because it was a gift from Kevin—she liked the weight of it against her thigh, the sense of security.

Jade sat with her face in her hands and imagined exploring the magical world of Athanasia. After talking one night in the barn about the Emerald Tablet, she had gladly made a deal with Kevin and Tim to return there. It would probably take eons to explore, even though time seemed to be slowed by a multiple of nine hours. When Tim and Kevin had entered Athanasia for the second time they were there for eight hours, which equaled seventy-two hours in standard Earth time: therefore, one Athanasia hour must equal nine earth hours. If they explored Athanasia for one week; that would mean they would be gone for sixty-three days.

Nine weeks. It would have to wait though, because her dad was the priority. Anyway, they could quite possibly be back within the hour with her dad.

To distract her thoughts, Jade took her notebook from her backpack and flicked through to a blank page, while musing on the idea of a multiverse, a fascinating and distracting concept. She breathed a sigh of relief, envisioning the infinite possibilities of a multiverse and each one had Kevin in it. He no longer needed to pass through the world of Athanasia to travel to the other side of the earth. While in a catacomb in the Middle East, after tapping into Shaun's head and emotions, Kevin said that's when he realized he could open portals to anywhere in the world as long as he had access to an emotionally-charged memory of the location.

At some point, while floating through her stream of consciousness, the sun came out.

"Earth to Jade," Kevin said, casting a shadow over her.

She blushed. Her tummy did somersaults, but for all the wrong reasons. *Something's not right, I feel frightened,* she thought. His mom, holding one of the twins, hugged him. Molly was playing hide and seek around the carcass of the plane with Kath. Once Molly saw Kevin, she raced over and he bent down to give her a big hug.

Kevin stood upright and tucked his fringe behind his ear, and said, "Ready?"

"Ready," Jade said. Feeling unsure as she dusted off her pants.

Sophia hugged Jade and whispered, "If you need our help, reach out to me with your mind."

Jade thought her feelings were hidden from the others, but obviously not from everyone.

"Don't worry, I haven't said anything. Remember the peace in the wind. Look for the light of the morning star," Sophia said, giving her another hug. Jade smiled and gave her a friendly push. "That's what my great-grandmother used to say."

NAUSEA, BILE, TREMORS AND FEAR FILLED JADE'S BEING. SHE began to sweat profusely as if she had a fever. Her heart raced as if danger was stalking her. She was scared for her life. She stumbled forward to the portal, resisting the urge to flee while blood pulsed at her temples. As her legs buckled, she grabbed her mother's hand, and they walked up to the front door where Kevin had placed the opening.

Her left foot touched the soothing, scintillating energy. It was beautiful, priceless. Warmth raced up her leg into her abdomen as her hands, arms, and chest were immersed in the embryonic energy. She became one with the endless. Her mind cleared. She was free of anxiety, and pain. She didn't want to leave the portal. A pleasant, intoxicating smell filled her senses, and her heart expanded with compassion. Kevin's hand pierced the membrane, reaching for her arm. The knowledge that she was no longer holding her mom's hand seeped into her being. Her mom was already on the other side and Kevin drew her toward him. She emerged out of the portal into her house in Myrtle Beach, South Carolina, USA.

Jade half expected the kitchen to smell of burned toast. But it was deathly quiet, dark and odorless. It seemed like it was the middle of the night with the air being humid, and the atmosphere thick.

Her mother flicked on the light switch. Plates, cups, knives, and forks lay in the sink. It was so unlike her father. Ants trailed from the window and over the dirty dishes. The air in the house had a stale, life- less taste. She looked down the hallway to her bedroom at the end of the corridor to see the door was closed, but she remembered leaving it open. It seemed like an eternity since she was last there. Her mother was looking around in wonderment.

"It's still the same," her mom said, touching the wall.

Kevin hovered in the doorway, respecting their space. Jade reached for his hand, and together they walked to the front door. They fixed their eyes on each other. She was apprehensive about opening the door and stepping outside.

"Well, what are you waiting for?" Kevin said. "What if there's nothing beyond the door?"

Kevin put his hand in the middle of the wooden door and waited. "It's quiet," he said. "It feels like an empty sealed jar."

"What do you mean," Jade said.

"It's waiting for something to fill it."

"With what?"

"People, animals, life," Kevin said. Jade reached for the door handle.

"Slow down. Stop and think for a minute. What was it like the last time you were on the porch?" Kevin said.

"Sunny."

"What did you see?"

"The old American Indian man was under the tree burning herbs in his seashell."

"Okay. Open the door. Hold that image in your mind."

Jade pulled the door toward her and raised her hand to turn on the porch light.

"No, leave it off."

Kevin pulled the door all the way open and pushed the screen door outward for Jade to step outside. "Think of the tree."

"I can't see anything. There is nothing here," she whispered. Her body filled with panic.

"Wait for your eyes to adjust."

With her hands outstretched, feeling for the handrail, Jade shuffled forward. The streetlights should be on, stars should be bright in the sky. It must be cloudy. The dark silhouette of the tree emerged from the night. "I see it," she said, and then the rain started. It poured down. Lightning cut across the sky showing abandoned cars parked along the street. The neighborhood looked staged. The house shook while thunder rolled overhead and out to the ocean.

Under the tree, the old man sat. A fire raged with life, despite the downpour. She turned to Kevin. "You see that?"

He looked as confused as she. "I see a tree. It wasn't there a minute ago."

The ill-at-ease feelings returned and Jade warily walked down the two steps, into the rain and across the road. The old man stood. "I am Chief Thundercloud. Come to the river of Great Turtle's forefathers where their spirits live among us. And you will find your father in the Realm of Lost Souls."

Jade reached the fire. There was no heat. Her head was light.

Dizzy, she swayed as if to the sound of a distant drum.

"I don't understand?" She was feeling nauseous. "Where is he?" Her skin was clammy and pale. It was such a short time since she had emerged from the portal, buzzing with energy, and now she felt like shit again.

Kevin had followed her into the rain and stood beside her. He touched her hand. "Jade, no one's there."

"What?" She blinked. The fire was gone, along with the old man. "But how? What do you think he meant?"

"Who? Nobody is there, Jade. I didn't hear anything. I saw the tree, but that's it."

Ignoring the feeling of her hair sticking to her face and the rain pelting down, Jade stared at Kevin. "He was right here," she said, walking around the tree. Her eyes had acclimatized to the dark and she could see behind her house, the mountains in the distance as if they had just descended from the sky. "What the hell is happening, K? How could you not see him? Tell me you can see the mountains behind us?" She didn't turn but glanced over her shoulder, indicating where he should look.

"Come on," Kevin said, putting a protective arm around her as they crossed the street.

"Jade!" her mother called from the porch. "What are you doing?" "The old man. He was here," Jade said, running across the street with Kevin.

"What? No one's there," her mom said. "So I've heard!"

"He said Dad is lost in the Realm of Lost Souls." "Maybe she had a vision," Kevin said.

The rain stopped and the clouds parted. The stars shone in the velvety night sky.

"I don't have visions!" Jade said, entering the house.

Jade grabbed two towels from the linen cupboard. She tossed one to Kevin. "He said his name was Chief Thundercloud. He started showing up when mom went missing. He said to go to the river of Great Turtle's ancestors."

The dizziness and nausea had dissipated. Her body felt as if it was on fire when she spoke of the old man, but she was now thinking it was from the soaked winter clothes she wore.

"Great Turtle forbade us to talk of the world of shadows. It is a world where you can lose your soul," her mom said.

"Where are all the people?" Kevin said. "There was no one on the streets. I couldn't feel a single emotion."

Jade went to her bedroom and picked out some of her favorite clothes to wear. Glowing on her bedroom wall were the pictures of the green door with the Seal of Solomon. The two-dimensional image looked three-dimensional. *What's going on?* And why would her dad be in trouble if he went with the old man? Why would the old man appear to her? There were too many questions she couldn't answer. *This is so frustrating. The world is just as crazy if not worse than before the return of the Emerald Tablet – the second Big Bang.*

Still standing in the hallway, Kevin dried himself off. "Do you know where the river is?" he asked before vigorously drying his hair.

"No, do you, Mom?" Jade said, putting the blue towel over her head and walking toward the bathroom with her pile of dry clothes. She put her clothes down on top of the vanity and held the door open.

"I'm not sure, but our ancestors, before they joined the Catawba Nation, were the Wateree peoples, which means 'to float on water'. The river is over two hours away."

Jade looked at Kevin. "Do you think you can get us there?" "Not unless you guys have been there before?"

"Mom, have we?" Jade was doing her best to keep it together. She closed the bathroom door, and quickly stripped off her winter gear. The wet clothes seemed to weigh a ton. She felt so fatigued. Pulling on a pair of dry olive green cargos, she toppled over, and managed to catch herself on the edge of the bath narrowly avoiding hitting her head on the side of the vanity.

Her head had started aching soon after they started talking about her ancestors. She was ashamed she never sought out her heritage. She was always proud of Great

Turtle, who was loved by the many believers who traveled far to see her. But now wasn't the time for regrets. They had to find her father and fast. She quickly changed her bra and put on her blue V-neck t-shirt that had a picture of an atom with *never trust an atom, they make up everything* written underneath. Jade kicked her wet clothes into a corner and left the bathroom.

"We haven't been to Wateree River, but when you were about two years old your dad and I took you and your great-grandmother to the Black Mountains. Your great-grandmother would strap you to her chest and take you on long walks and you two would be gone for hours."

Her legs were becoming heavy again, and she started to sweat. Swirls of energy were rising up from her solar plexus and around her, creating a feeling of expansiveness. *This must be what Sophia sometimes experiences*, Jade thought.

"Are you okay?" Kevin reached for Jade as she started to fall.

Her mother caught her other arm. Together they helped her to the dining room table.

"Maybe a glass of water will help," Kevin said, going into the kitchen. He turned back, looking over the breakfast bar. "Where do you keep your glasses?"

"Top left-hand cupboard." Kevin didn't move.

Cupboard, K, left-hand side, she thought.

He cocked his head to the side, focusing on the air around her. "What are you seeing?" asked Ellen. "Your mother told me about your second sight. Why are you looking at Jade like that? What do you see?"

"I don't normally see things; it's just a knowing or an overwhelming emotion."

"You're a clairsentient, Kevin," Ellen said.

"Hmm. She is surrounded by green light, and her bracelet is glowing, but ..."

"But what, K?" Jade said, feeling nervous.

"It's weird. I see your veins filled with white light."

Ellen stepped back trying to see what Kevin saw. "Jade, maybe you should rest awhile?"

"There's no time to rest. Anyway, I think I would go stir-crazy doing nothing."

"An energy drink is what you need." Her mom opened the pantry doors and disappeared inside, reappearing with three bottles. "Kevin, can you pop these in your backpack?"

Jade accepted a bottle from her mom and took a big drink, then stowed it in her backpack. "I feel so uncomfortable, like something's wrong. Nothing feels alive, it's like we are on a movie set. Can you guys smell anything? Can you hear anything? Nothing seems real. We *have* to leave." The wind rattled the windows.

"Relax, Jade. Worrying won't help," Ellen said. "Kevin, check the garage for the car. Jade, you stay here while I get my camel pack." Her mom darted into the laundry and searched the cupboards for her hiking gear.

Kevin zipped up his bag. He flicked on the tap and filled a glass of water. Cautiously, he sipped the water. He spat it back out into the sink. "Sorry," he said, wiping his mouth with the back of his hand. "It tastes stale. I think I'll pass." He pulled off his windbreaker and removed his jumper. He then put the windbreaker back on. Smiling, Jade watched his movements. He was five feet, eight inches tall and cute. "Why did you put your jacket back on? It's not raining anymore." She watched Kevin put down the glass.

He backed into the kitchen and headed for the side door. "It's going to rain again. The wind's blowing a gale."

"How do you know it's going to rain? And how do you know that's the garage door?"

"It just is. And that's the most likely one," he said.

He opened the door. No car. "There are three bicycles?"

Jade was up out of her chair, heading after her mom. "Mom, have you got a picture of the time when we were at the Wateree River?"

"You read my mind," she said. "It's not of Wateree River, but I have a photo of us at Black Mountain. We stayed in one of the lodges. The Catawba River is maybe a day's hike. The Catawba flows into the Wateree." Mom handed the picture to Kevin.

He had a cheeky grin on his face. Jade stood closer to see the photo. "Mom, really, is that the only picture you've got?" The happy snap was of her parents sitting at a picnic table with Jade lying on a blanket butt naked and smiling straight at the camera.

2

In the palm of Kevin's hand, the photo began to suddenly glow with light. A crackling and a familiar hum filled the room. The white light grew into a portal, the kitchen disappeared, and Jade was absorbed by the healing membrane.

Sedate and graceful, her body's natural healing system fired into action, and she never gave a thought to breathe as she moved through the portal. Once again, her troubles melted away. She stretched her arms outward and floated; listening and imagining the campground in the photo. A memory and feeling of being bounced around in a baby harness, attached to Great Turtle, came to her. Great Turtle having an animated discussion with a white deer.

The image faded as she emerged from the beautiful space of the portal, and into the foreboding darkness of a forest.

There was an absence of wind and any smell of the recent rainfall, along with a lack of dampness on the plants or a twinkle of dew. The clouds parted, and a full moon was revealed.

"Why are the trees so – still?" Kevin asked. "Close your eyes," her mom said.

"Why?" Jade asked frowning. "Trust me, Jade."

Jade closed her eyes, and the overwhelming silence hijacked her brain. "I can't do this," she said, opening her eyes. "I'm too wired." She pushed a phantom strand of hair off her face, tightened her ponytail, and pushed her bracelet up her forearm.

Her mother reached out and took Jade's hands. "Close your eyes and relax."

Jade let go of her mom's hands. She shuffled her feet in the decomposing leaves and tugged the bottom of her blue shirt down.

"Just do it," Kevin said. "What are you afraid of?"

Jade found Kevin's eyes in the shadow of his face. "I'm not afraid." Jade wiped her hands down her cargo pants and buttoned up a side pocket, before touching her bowie knife. She took her mom's hands and closed her eyes. "Okay. What now?"

"Close your eyes and listen to my voice," her mom said. "Breath in through your nose and out through your mouth to the count of three, like you are breathing out through a straw. Good. Again, breathe in calm for the count of three and breathe out the stress. And again ..."

Jade felt herself settling, her shoulders dropped, and her body began to relax.

"Recall a warm spring night, and the last time you felt the wind blowing your hair, Jade. Listen for the sound of the wind passing through the trees, and relax ... That's it, Jade."

Her body began to sway, moved by the imagined wind. Her mother's voice was faint, telling her to squeeze her hands, to stretch her shoulders back and slowly open her eyes. She didn't want to open her eyes: it felt as if she had only just closed them. The sensation in her body was a little like the energy in the portal membrane. Her mom tapped her elbow twice.

"Jade, open your eyes," Kevin said softly.

Jade's consciousness rose to the surface from a depth she was unaware she had traveled to, and she wrestled to open her eyes. She raised her eyebrows as if they had the power to pull her lids up.

"Stay relaxed. Keep noticing the wind. Stay calm. Slowly peek through slits before completely opening your eyes." Her mother's voice was soft and soothing.

Jade remembered a time when she was seven: it was the first time she had seen Great Turtle conducting a healing ceremony. Jade had fallen asleep, and when she woke, she had barely opened her eyes— only peeking through narrow slits. What she had seen frightened her. She couldn't move. It was the first time she had experienced sleep paralysis and it was terrible. She had wanted to curl into herself and retract from consciousness. Spirits had danced in the fire and floated in the sky. They had made her feel so anxious she had quickly closed her eyes and drifted back to sleep as she told herself it had only been a dream.

Her mother woke her now with the same tone—kind, caring and reassuring. Jade timidly opened her eyes and saw the forest had come to life. She turned around, looking up at the canopy. A gentle wind moved through the trees and the all sounds of life awakened. Fresh air filled her lungs.

Kevin, with a torch pointing down at the ground, was sitting against a tree as if he had been waiting for a while.

"How much time has passed?" She looked for the moon.

Kevin aimed the torch at his watch. "You're obsessed with time;" he said, tapping his granddad's watch. "About half an hour."

"Impossible," she said. "It was like three minutes."

"Nope, it was thirty. You experienced phenomenal time, that's all. What I want to know," Kevin said, brushing himself off, "is how did you make the forest breathe?"

"What? Don't be ridiculous. Trees don't inhale or exhale. I didn't make anything happen." She looked around and toward her mother, but as she did, she felt liberation, a freedom from within the forest, as if it did inhale and exhale.

"Why are you so snappy," Kevin said.

"I'm ... did I?" Jade frowned at her mom. "What just happened?

That's impossible."

"How do you feel?" her mother asked. "Calm and relaxed?" "Yes."

"That's good, and that's all that matters."

Jade whipped around toward a sound. Her legs were a little stiff from standing in one position for so long. "What was that?"

Through the trees, Jade could see a faint light in the distance. She moved cautiously. "K, mom. Can you see the light? Over there," she said, pointing between the trees. Jade wasn't going to assume they could each see the same things any more.

"Yes," her mom said, moving a little toward it. "Yeah, me too," Kevin said.

"K, do you think anybody is in there?" Jade said.

"We haven't run into anybody yet. Honestly, I don't know if I want too. I'm not sure if I'm ready to trust anybody outside our group..." His voice trailed off as if he sensed something.

"It is possible. We did see a few people in the UK," Jade's mom said.

"Maybe we should check it out," Kevin suggested.

"Did you bring a gun?" Jade's mom asked Kevin.

"No. Did you? What would I need a gun for? I assumed the target practice was for hunting food, if necessary," Kevin said. "I've got my bowie knife and Jade's got hers. I'm sensing fear, other than my own. Be cautious, but let's move a tad closer, and see if what I'm picking up grows stronger."

Jade moved closer to the source of the light.

"We can sneak up, suss out whatever it is, and if there's no sign of my dad, we backtrack out of here," Jade said.

"Okay. Let's hurry," Kevin said.

With a note of apprehension, her mom said, "Jade, lead the way."

Without replying, Jade began to thread her way quietly through the trees. Kevin's hand on her arm made her stop. He put a finger to his lips. She kept still and concentrated. In the distance, she could see a campground. The light shone through a window in a wooden building that had a sweeping veranda. She heard twigs snapping. "K, what is it?"

Before he could answer, three men with rifles stepped from the bushes. Kevin raised his torch, blinding them. Two looked like brothers in their early twenties, and the other, a much older man could be their father. The two brothers had enough dead rabbits hanging over their shoulders to feed a small army. She was surprised she hadn't smelled their approach. They must be the owners of the emotions Kevin had picked up. Her mom grabbed her hand and pulled her to her side. Kevin stood his ground, and took a defensive stance in front of her. He kept his torch beam aimed at the men as if it was as powerful as their guns.

"Sorry to frighten you, ma'am," the old guy said, lowering his weapon, "but my boys here have been telling a fantastical tale about the howling wind stopping in its tracks and the air turning stale. And when it did two women and a young man appeared out of thin air. I couldn't believe the story, and neither did anybody else, so I just had to look for myself. I have to give the boys some credit—the air was tasting a bit stale, and all the little critters had hushed. It was downright eerie. Where did you all come from?"

Everyone else? That means there are others. Strange to see people close up again, but it was great to hear a southern accent. Jade wanted to reach out and touch them to be sure they were real.

"Do ya mind getting that light out of my face, boy? Ma'am, we don't intend to hurt you. How long has it been since you've seen any folk? You're mighty skittish."

"Kevin, lower your torch," Her mom said.

Kevin did as she asked and pointed his torch to the ground, casting the men in a halo of light.

"It has been a while. Do mind asking your boys to lower their weapons?" Jade said.

"Oh, so you're a local," the old man said. "Boys, lower them guns."

"What if they're infected, Pa?" The younger of the two boys was wearing a Yankees baseball cap and looked to be in his early twenties. They both were wearing fatigue jackets.

"They're not infected, son. They wouldn't have been so polite. They would've taken our guns before we knew what had happened and blown our heads off," the old man said. "Now lower them guns."

"We're from Myrtle Beach," Jade's mom said. "We're

looking for Chief Thundercloud. My husband, Scott, is with him."

"The last time we saw my dad was about seven months ago," Jade said.

"We don't care who you're looking for. You should just keep on moving. You can't come to the lodge. We had a couple of people walk out of the forest, before the whiteout. But they'd been camping in the mountains hiding out from the infected. You don't look like you've been roughing it. You really ain't infected, are you?"

"No, we're not infected," Jade said.

"Cause you're the second group of people since the whiteout. And the first group after the whiteout was a mistake," said the old man.

Jade thought the whiteout had just encompassed Casey's estate, but perhaps the whole world had been affected.

"Alright, then. How'd you get here, and what are you doing in the woods after dark? You're taking a hell of a risk."

"Like my mom said, we're looking for my father," Jade snapped. "He went missing a couple of weeks before the whiteout. We believe he went with Chief Thundercloud. My great-grandmother is Great Turtle."

That seemed to mean something to them. The young boy looked at the older man and then at his brother. He lowered his gun.

"Well, then, it's best you all come with us to the lodge and meet the others. Friends and family of Great Turtle are welcome. Anything you need little lady, it's yours."

He didn't wait for them to answer. He walked off into the darkness toward the light, and his two sons followed.

Jade, confused, lowered her voice. "Let's just get out of here?" "Kevin, what did you pick up?" her mom said. "Any malice?" "Fear, mostly. They're scared of us. It was them I was sensing.

When you mentioned Great Turtle, there was a surge of gratitude, masking the fear."

"Are you guys going to keep chatting back there, or are you going to join us for supper? There are a lot of folks who would like to meet the relatives of Great Turtle. But I'm not sure if anyone will know anything about your man, Scott.

"Okay," her mom said. "We'll come for a while. Then we'll need to be on our way. We have to find Chief Thunder-cloud and Scott."

As they approached the main house, they could hear the sounds of laughter, and the aromas of a hearty meal. Jade followed the men up the steps to the sweeping veranda and the men stamped the dirt from their boots before entering the house. The youngest brother closed the front door after Kevin and her mom entered the foyer. It was homely. The chairs were worn, and covered with cushions and throw rugs for extra comfort—and perhaps to protect the fabric beneath. The coffee tables were littered with magazines and the walls were lined with book shelves. Card tables with games half-played were pushed up against the shelves. A cabinet for holding firearms was by the front door. The men placed their guns in the cabinet and the eldest of the two brothers walked to a chessboard on a card table, then moved the white rook. The men disappeared into another room and the noise of many people dining wafted through.

"Wait in here," the old man instructed as they followed him into what could be described as a mess hall. A large table against the far wall displayed a modest buffet. There were ten tables that could each seat eight people, but only six tables were full.

"Everybody, my boys haven't been smoking the funny weed after all." A couple of people laughed. "These are the three people my boys saw. I'd like to introduce you to ..." He looked at her mom.

"Ellen. This is my daughter, Jade, and her friend, Kevin."

Everyone stopped eating, and fell silent. The people were tense and rigid and had forgotten about their laughter and food. One man started yelling. "What are you doing bringing strangers into the safe zone? I thought we all agreed, no more strangers were allowed in until they prove their worthiness. How do you know they're not gonna slit our throats in the middle of the night?"

"Sit down, Mac, you've had a bit too much moonshine," said the man. "Ellen, Jade and Kevin, my name is Russell, but you can call me Russ. And these fine men are my two boys, Mitch and Bob. See the fine lady over there?" he said, pointing to a woman sitting two tables away from the buffet.

"That's my wife, and the young girl next to her is Ruby, my daughter." He looked back at the man he called Mac, who was still standing, waiting for a valid response, and said, "This woman, Ellen, and her daughter are the descendants of Great Turtle. Do you think they qualify to be here, Mac?"

Russell's wife stood up, but her daughter Ruby tried to pull her back into the chair. Mac was still standing. He touched his chair, and just as Jade thought he was going to sit down again, he hurried toward her mom. Jade, worried, looked at Kevin. He put his hand over his bowie knife. Jade unclipped the strap on her blade and went to step in front of her mom. Before she could react, Mac extended his hand. Russell's wife greeted her husband with a kiss. Then without a word, the woman embraced her. Jade watched as her mom allows the woman to continue to hug her. The woman looked at Jade and said, "You look like her. You can stay as long as you like. Are you hungry? Can I get you something to eat?"

Mac said, "Yes, you must eat with us. Take my chair." "There are plenty of chairs, Mac," Russell said.

There were murmurs. Some stood. A few headed over to the newcomers before Russell intervened.

He put up his hand. "Now everybody, please take your seats and resume eating your dinner. Don't put our guests under any pressure... all in good time." He turned to Jade and her mom. "They just want to thank you for all the goodness Great Turtle brought them before she moved into the spirit world."

Russell's wife smiled at them. "My name is Sue," she said

as she took Ellen's hand. She pointed to her daughter. "My Ruby wouldn't be here today if it wasn't for your grand-mother. I had a difficult pregnancy. Great Turtle saved her life," she said, meeting Jade's eyes. "Many people in this camp can tell you how she helped them. Mitch, why don't you give some rabbit stew to Jade and Kevin."

"Follow us to the buffet table, and you can help yourself to something to eat," said Mitch, leading them across the room.

"Hey guys, do you want to leave your gear by the door?" Bob asked Kevin.

"No, I'm good," said Kevin.

"Me too." Jade was reluctant to separate from her mom. They had to get back on track and find her dad.

"This group of deadbeats are okay," Mitch said, passing a group of young adults. "There's rabbit stew, bread, fruit, cheese, water and juice. Take a plate and dig in."

Jade took a piece of bread and goats' milk cheese. Kevin did the same, but also poured himself a glass of juice. They were guided back to sit with the group he'd called deadbeats.

"That's Noah with the black shirt, next to him is Jackson and Charlie, across from Charlie is Emma, Steve, and Mason."

There was a guy at the other end of the table that Mitch didn't introduce who kept eating his dinner. Now that she thought about it, she'd noticed him when they first arrived, but he'd paid no attention to them at all. The guy glanced at Steve and Mason. They stood up, took their food, and went to sit at another table. Bob dragged a chair from another table and put it at the end.

"Sorry about Mac," Mitch said, "but a few months ago, we had a full house." He scanned the room. "Soon after the whiteout cleared, it snowed. It was absolutely freezing, never seen it so cold in all my life. We had twice as many people taking refuge up here from the virus. Some of the old ones died from the cold, but most of them were murdered. A group of nine men and a pregnant woman came out of the woods, bearing gifts. They had a recent kill – three deer – and they wanted to share. We let them in. They seemed kind, harmless so we built a fire and had a feast. We let them occupy two of the cabins. The woman stayed in the main house, which seemed a bit strange at the time. We thought she must be the partner of one of the men. When mom asked her if she wanted to stay with the single women in the big house, she jumped at the chance.

"One night the nine men woke and started killing people as they slept. Slit their throats. They had planned to take the women from the start. Our women fought back, but a lot of them were killed. They had them chained together ready to flee, god knows where. Mac was the first to raise the alarm. He fired the first few rounds taking out a couple of the men. Crazy Bear, that's Noah, he got the next one, and I got off a couple of shots myself. When they arrived, they had seemed like good folk. Mac had said to shoot them; said he had an inkling, and Great Turtle always told him to listen to his inklings. But, because he was always drunk, we ignored him," Mitch said.

"But Mac was right," Bob said. "Those of us that can shoot have been teaching the rest how to shoot to kill. The virus may be gone, but people are still people, and when they get desperate and afraid, well..."

"Tomorrow," Bob said, looking at Jade. "I can show you around. I like your blade. If you want, we can teach you how to shoot."

"That's kind, but no thanks," Jade said. "We're heading out tonight."

"Give it up, Bob. Can't you see she's not interested?" A blond girl with a tattoo of a butterfly on her wrist said, without looking up from her food.

Jade tried to recall her name... Cheryl... no, Charlie. "Thanks, Bob, but we've got to keep moving to find Chief Thundercloud and my dad. We have to find the Catawba River to lead us to the Wateree River."

"Your friend doesn't talk much, does he?" Mitch said, looking at Kevin.

"If your father is out there, he doesn't have much chance of surviving. Maybe you should stay here," Charlie said, glancing up.

"Charlie's right. You shouldn't be out at night," Bob said. "We've heard some peculiar sounds coming from the forest."

"Like what?" Kevin said.

"Like bears roaring and moaning as if they are being attacked. Cubs bawling for their mothers; wailing women, screaming; the sound of whistling wind when there is no wind. The animals go crazy. And just now, the world froze. The forest stood still for close to thirty minutes. Then we saw you lot. Mitch and I wouldn't have been caught dead out there if we hadn't seen you guys appear."

"By the way," Mitch said, pushing his bowl aside and wiping his mouth with the back of his hand. "You haven't explained how you got here. First, I thought you were witches because you magically appeared. We've heard the wailing of women and the cackling of children, the echoes of dying men from the battlefields of history. The dead haunt the dark nights. We think there might be witches about, conjuring up the dead," Mitch said, looking at them questioningly.

"Come on, Mitch, stop trying to scare them. She's Great Turtle's descendant," Bob said. "But he's right. The night belongs to the dead. That's all I'm going to say."

At the head of the table, the guy that Mitch didn't introduce previously, was watching over the rim of his coffee cup. He had the most appealing blue eyes Jade had ever seen. She tried not to look at him directly, but he just kept staring at her. He wore a copper bracelet similar to hers. His hair was as black as night, similar to hers. Dangling from around his neck on a piece of leather was a chunk of quartz. He had a tattoo on his right wrist, but she couldn't quite make out what it was. There was something unique about this guy; he had such an air of authority. The girl, Charlie, sitting next to him, kept looking at Jade, then touching his wrist. She looked a little jealous.

"You serious? That's freaky, it sounds like a nightmare. But we have to leave," Jade said. "We're heading out tonight."

"Well then, that settles it," said Mr. Blue Eyes.

3
_____

The energy at the table and the mood in the room lifted. The surviving Black Mountains community was in good spirits. Kevin was talking casually with Emma and Jackson about their knives. Jade noticed Charlie was whispering to Noah and making him frustrated. He too, had a tattoo on his wrist, a black bear.

"Why the tattoos?" Jade asked moving forward to get a closer look at the bear.

"They're our spirit animals," Noah said stroking his bear. "It reminds me that the power of the bear is my strength. Whenever I see, think, or feel the energy of a bear I know I have to quiet my mind and go within myself to the womb-cave, to align with the energies of Mother Earth. I will be nourished from the placenta of the Great Void and only then, will I find answers to my questions. But once you're in the

Dream Lodge seeking the womb-cave, you'd better know what you are doing and have a good anchor in this realm, or you can come back as mad as a hatter. Or worse, trapped between consciousness and unconsciousness forever."

"Do you only have one spirit animal?" Jade asked.

"No. All seven totem animals are your spirit animals. But one defines you more than the others," Charlie said.

"What does the butterfly mean?" Jade asked Charlie.

"The power of the butterfly is the ability to know and change the mind," Charlie said.

"And she changes her mind constantly," Noah quipped.

Charlie nudged him with her elbow. "Don't listen to him. It's about understanding cycles and self-transformation."

Jade noticed a few people quietly hanging around behind her, waiting for her to finish eating and talking. As soon as she had finished, one by one, they politely excused themselves before hugging her.

A pregnant woman came up to her and said, "I didn't know Great Turtle, but will you bless my baby with good health."

She didn't know what to say or do so she smiled. "May the light of Great Spirit shine from your daughter's heart," Jade was horrified. She had no idea why she said that. Oh god, she was so embarrassed. Everyone was looking at her, including Mr. Blue Eyes.

"It's a girl?" The woman looked happy with the proposition.

Jade excused herself and went over to her mom. "We

have to go," she whispered in her ear. "I can't do this. You can stay, it's okay truly, but I have to go."

Her mom met her eyes. "I need a couple of minutes. Your dad is not here; but, this couple said they met Chief Thundercloud along the trail. He was searching for his son's family who actually passed through a week later, heading to the Devil's Tower. They said Chief Thundercloud was traveling with a man that fits your dad's description. He called him professor, so that could be him; but, it was before the whiteout. Give me a few minutes to find out if they know which direction they went and I'll meet you outside."

Jade smiled at the couple. "It's nice to meet you," she told them, and left for the exit.

Mr. Blue Eyes had left the table and disappeared into a side room. When he reappeared, she was already heading out into the foyer. Each step seemed to echo in the dining hall, but it was taking so long to get out. Jade was grateful Kevin was right behind her. When Mr. Blue Eyes passed Kevin and caught up with her in the foyer, he stopped her from opening the doors to the outside. Charlie was on his heels right as he seized her wrists and turned them over, looking for something. He touched the copper bracelet and then let go, then pulled out a pamphlet from his back pocket. He handed her a map and said, "Take this map. And stay on the trail. My name is Mingan. Good luck, Raven Wings." He turned and left.

As her mom joined them, she asked, "Mom, how does

Mingan know the spiritual name given to me by Great Turtle?"

"A lot of people here knew your great-grandmother. Maybe she mentioned it."

Jade walked into the night, heading for the trail. Her mom was talking about some of the people she met. Jade was deep in her own thoughts; she couldn't stop thinking about Mingan. How did he know her name? And why had he been staring at her? Was she just being paranoid? She stopped in mid-stride.

"Did you hear that?" Jade said, whispering. "Someone called my name." She strained her head forward, listening.

Kevin adjusted the straps of his backpack. "I didn't hear anything, although I could feel energy flowing through you like warm honey. But I know you're feeling confused, fuzzy, and maybe even a little paranoid."

She ignored Kevin. "Mom, did you hear it?" "No," her mom said.

"Never mind," Jade said, frustrated.

Kevin was looking at her curiously, waiting for her to move. She fixed her eyes on him, challenging his stare, but he was unflinching. She blushed, and turned away, suddenly grateful for the night.

Jade was the driving force, and they were going to follow her. But where was she leading them? A positive flow of energy didn't beckon her. Instead, she felt a dark, thick, life-less energy—of a place she never wanted to go to. Just the thought of it made her tense and grind her teeth. The moment of feeling calm was gone. Her heart was racing. Her chest was filled with heat. *Okay, relax*, she told herself.

Kevin was beside her, still waiting patiently for her to point the way.

Without warning, the sound of her father calling her name came from far beyond the trees. It reminded her of playing hide-and-seek with him, and she would hide in the basement. Jade shivered.

The birds were silent. Her shoulders rose to her ears as she cringed. His voice was as clear as if he stood right beside her, which was impossible. She was scared. This was no childhood game and he wasn't hiding. He was trapped, but where? And why could she hear him? Was she losing her mind?

To follow a feeling, to listen to sounds and voices no one else could hear, wasn't logical. To go beyond logic was still foreign to her, but she couldn't ignore her father calling.

"Are you sure you didn't hear anything?" she said, searching her mother's face. Why was he calling out to her and not her mom? Maybe because he doesn't know she's alive?

"This way," she said, with sudden urgency and renewed hope.

The light from Kevin's torch bounced around, lighting up the trail ahead as he walked beside her. Her mom, who was very quiet, was so close behind that Jade could hear her breathing as they tackled the terrain in the dark. She listened intently for crickets, cicadas, and frogs, the usual suspects to allude that a river might be nearby. At the same time, her ears ached from the influx of silence, while the drum-like pounding of her blood made it difficult to hear anything. The smells of dew, animal excrement and different trees and plants filled her senses and she could even taste the various plants. As she inhaled, it was like chewing on bark. A state of effervescence filled her being. Every one of her senses was rising to new levels, awakened by the song of the forest.

After about twenty minutes of silent travel, Kevin said, "You look like you've lost something, what are you trying to find?" He stopped and waited for an answer.

His voice boomed inside her head. Shocked, Jade fell hard from her lofty experience back into reality.

"My dad," she said as if coming out of sleep. "What else?" "The river," her mother answered for her, "the river."

"Do *you* know which way to go?" Jade snapped. But why would her mother hang behind and let Jade stumble through the woods if she knew which way to go? Jade knew she was blindly lashing out, but she couldn't do anything to stop herself.

"And what planet are *you* from, Kevin. This is all about finding my dad. I expected him to be at the house. I didn't expect to be hiking through the mountains looking for an apparition who knows where my father is. And Mom, if your big scientific brain knows where we have to go, then please, take the lead!" Jade made a sweeping gesture with her arm and stepped aside. "If not, then why are you here? What are you good for?" She could feel deep within her that she had gone too far, and she didn't mean any of it. She was frustrated, but something was triggering her. "And what was that back there? Huh! How did you put me in a trance state? That's what it was, wasn't it?"

"I know who you are and who you will become," her mom said. "You're heading in the right direction, Jade, and you have a profound look of concentration. I've seen that look before. Kevin jolted you and you're now irritated because you came back too quickly."

"Back from where? I'm right here, Mom! I haven't gone anywhere."

"You're being rude," Kevin said. "You're on edge."

Kevin nudged her shoe with his, and she could feel the gentle flow of his energy. She drew in a deep breath. "I'm freaking out because I'm worried I'm going to get us all lost or killed in the process of finding him."

"We can't get lost. I can always get us home," he said, tapping the side of his head.

"Shh," Jade said. "Did you hear that?" Leaves and twigs being compressed to her right... something moved through the brush.

As a bear ambled out from behind the bushes, Jade tilted her head down. She recalled what Noah had said about quieting his mind when he saw a bear, but did he mean when he metaphorically sees a bear, or a real flesh and blood bear. Random images invaded her mind of a black wolf, a white deer, a memory of gentle Great Turtle speaking to the same white deer years ago, the howl of distant wolves or coyotes, the light of the morning star in the sky, and stones with images painted on them.

A flash of light filled her vision, her breathing quickened. The rotating images accelerated like a merry-go-round, going faster and faster. It was hard to breathe and the light was so bright. The bear was so close she could smell wet fur and feel the warmth of its breath. It went black behind her eyes, the comfort of darkness filling her vision. Her eyes were opened. Kevin was in the darkness and her mother was in darkness. It had been Kevin's torch, that's all; Kevin's flashlight in her face, the light, the blinding golden light was Kevin. Her racing heart eased. Her breathing calmed. The sensation of being grounded was welcome. Kevin wrapped his pinky with hers, as she physically opened her eyes. It had been like awakening within a dream.

"Am I going mad?"

"What just happened?" Kevin said, letting go of her pinky.

"Where did the bear go?" Jade could still smell the fur and feel the warmth of its breath as she scanned the area around her. Kevin and her mom were so calm; but, under the circumstances they should be frantic.

Kevin stepped back, letting his fringe partially hide his blushing. He had a hint of sadness in his voice. "There was no bear that I saw. I felt the dizzy sensation of a roller coaster out of control. I saw a wolf, which reminded me of the black wolf that was about to tear you to pieces the day we met and I saw the white deer, the same one that guided me to you; the same white deer that had guided Shaun and visited Sophia. You saw those images too, didn't you? You feel White Deer, don't you? She's always been with you."

"We have to go this way." Jade didn't know the answers, and it was exasperating. What about the bear? Was it an illusion? She didn't understand the images she had seen with her mind's eye or how they got in her head. How was she going to explain it to someone else? Jade shouldered Kevin aside, ignoring the spark of electricity she felt between them. She wanted to keep moving and shut out the images entering her mind.

Follow the sound of the deer... it's White Deer; no, it's just a deer, she argued with herself pushing aside branches. It was only an average deer in an ordinary forest. Jade ambled onward, pretending she didn't feel anything and that the bear had no meaning.

The silence spooked her. It didn't matter how rational she was, or how powerful her inner voice was, she was scared. To distract herself from the eerie feelings, she calculated the probabilities and concluded she was getting closer to the river. Her body shuddered and the thoughts of spirit entities entered her mind. Ever since she was a child, she had been irrationally afraid of the spirit world and denied its existence. When she had first entered Athanasia, after seeing Great Turtle, Jade thought her fears had been alleviated. But, it wasn't the idea of spirits she was terrified of; it was the possibility of certain types of spirits her great-grandmother had spoken of she feared, the ones she now felt lurking just out of sight.

UNDERSTANDING SHE WAS ON A JOURNEY THAT REQUIRED HER to look for the unexplainable, Jade decided to be tenacious. She expanded her awareness in order to become receptive of any signs that would show her the way to the river where the spirit of Great Turtle's ancestors roamed, because right now, she was lost. Her spirit and mind were clouded. A mist moved hauntingly through the trees and the moon had disappeared. She looked behind her to find that her mother was gone and Kevin was gone.

"Mom, Kevin." Her voice was shaky. "Where are you guys? K?" The dry fog intensified. Frantic, she circled around looking for Kevin and her mom. Which way had she come? The trees loomed over her. Bats flew out of the canopy, a symbol of rebirth. A snake slithered nearby—transmutation. Another snake rustled in the underbrush on her right. She knew it wasn't possible, but in her mind's eye, she saw the reptile, with orange eyes, slithering toward her.

A warm light glowed through the fog. "Kevin, Mom, is that you?" "You shouldn't be here," a man said in a deep voice.

Jade stepped backward until she could feel the tree she knew was behind her. She waited to hear if the deep voice would speak again, then she forced herself to speak.

"Who's there? Who are you? Where am I?"

In the mist, silhouettes moved languidly. "You shouldn't be here." "Who, who said that?" She turned around confused, trying to pinpoint where the voice was originating from. "Wait. Stop."

They either didn't hear her, or were ignoring her pleas. An apparition of a solemn tribe of men, women and children from the 1700s came into view; they maintained a rhythmic stride and passed by. The people in the tribe looked lost, sad and tired, as if they'd been walking forever. Jade wrapped her arms around herself. *Don't faint, don't faint, it's not real.*

A deep resonance traveled through her body—a drummer, walking at the back of the group, was pounding a leather drum in time with her heartbeat. It was getting stronger as the group passed. The drummer was holding his drum high above his head. Are they really there? Or were they emotional imprints, like Casey had spoken about? *Are they the memories of the forest?* But the voice had definitely spoken directly to her.

She willed herself to move and rounded the tree until she was behind it. She backed away from the ghosts, but maybe she was also moving away from Kevin and her mom. Her feet made no noise, although there should've been a crunching sound as each foot pressed down on the fallen leaves. She cursed herself for getting lost. The dense fog engulfed her.

She visualized a rising sun and shuffled forward, blindly. An eagle in the night cried out above. A few feet away, White Deer, surrounded by a violet hue, penetrated the fog and stopped beside her. Jade reached out to stroke its back; the deer was soft and warm. Jade placed her hand on the back of its neck and felt its strong muscles. White Deer set the pace and the whiteout gradually began to clear. The scent of marshland filled her nose as she stepped out of the forest to the banks of the river.

The clouds passed, the moon shone and the indirect light revealed a bear fishing beyond the edge of tranquil waters. Introspection, she thought. All these thoughts kept popping into her mind. How could a bear make her think of the word introspection, a snake stimulating the idea of transmutation, a bat of rebirth? *Where was all this coming from?* Her previous annoyance for uncertainty lessened just a tad, because as she realized that not knowing everything about this world or her powers was okay. She'd learn.

The bear turned as if suddenly aware of her presence, but White Deer had vanished. The bear slowly walked toward her. *Oh shit, oh shit.* She slipped in the mud and scrambled to her feet, backing into a willow tree. She begged the fog to come back or a cloud to pass over the moon, so she could hide in the darkness. The bear stood on its back legs and sniffed the air. *Run, Jade, run,* she thought. She didn't move, but tried to become one with the tree. The grizzly dropped back down to all fours. It turned to the water and gave a sorrowful bellow that echoed across the river. Slowly, it headed downstream and Jade let out her breath.

"Jade!" Kevin called from the forest. "Over here," she said.

Before she stepped away from the tree, she rested her

hand on its trunk. "Thank you." She parted the willow's curtain of branches. She could see the approaching beam of light as Kevin darted between the trees jogging toward her.

Jade watched the bear jump over some rocks and disappear into the forest. White Deer was nowhere to be seen. Misty vapors drifted from the surface of the river. Jade knelt down and touched the fresh, silky water, calming her anxious heart.

"What happened to you?" Kevin asked.

Jade's mom appeared, gasping for air, and then reached out to hug Jade. "Let's rest," he said, watching Jade closely.

Kevin reached his arm over his shoulder and pulled his pack around to the front. He unfastened the clip and took out a bottle of lemon and lime and handed it to her. Their fingers touched as Jade took the bottle and she felt the sparks between them but said nothing. She was struggling to pull up the cap and went to use her teeth, but Kevin quickly took it and opened it. "Savage!" he said, smiling.

Jade smiled back.

"Something's changed. You're different, it's your aura. You're opening up. What happened?" His nose had scrunched up, and he gazed at Jade intensely. His worry and concern for Jade made him look older than his soon-to-be-sixteen years.

"It's hard to say. It's all incomprehensible. Freaky, actually. I'm not sure what's happening." She drank hard, the plastic bottle collapsing inward from the strength of her feverish consumption. "I needed that." She handed back the bottle and touched her stomach. "Or... maybe not so good." As refreshing as it was, it wasn't going to stay down. Quickly she turned to the side and puked. She couldn't understand why she was always feeling ill these days. She bent at the waist and threw up again.

"Small sips, Jade," her mother said, rubbing her back. "Your Great Turtle couldn't keep anything down before she entered certain healing states. That's how she knew the severity of the illness the person coming to see her was carrying."

Listening to the sounds of the night, Jade wondered where the world she called normal was. When they had returned from the tomb of Thoth, she thought life would go back to the way it had always been. This world was not the same, something was very different.

Wiping her mouth with the back of her hand, she had a compulsion to glance over her right shoulder at the river. Vapor floating off the water turned into spirits walking down the middle of the river. Jade perceived their sorrow and thought she heard weeping. "Why are they so sad?"

"Who?" said Kevin.

"Them!" she said, pointing to the middle of the river. "I thought you, of all people, would be doubled over with the overwhelming emotions. The dead are weeping. If they are in the so-called spirit world, why are they in pain? Why do they cry?"

"You can hear them?" her mom asked. "Your great-grandmother said one day you would become a healer and a seer."

"A shaman?" said Kevin.

"It's not something I want for you, because you can become a target of an envious shaman, alive or dead. She said you were a seer. You see the unseen realms. You are seeing them now, aren't you?"

"The bear!" Kevin said, more to himself than aloud.

But Jade heard him and knew what he was thinking. "I feel their sorrow. I hear their tears, but not with my ears; I hear them with my heart. The grief aches in my bones. They have suffered and were plagued with illness." She felt so cold she started to shiver. She arched forward and held herself tight. "I want to curl up like an armadillo because I feel help-less. I want to help them, but there are so many. If they are genuinely the spirits of people from the past, why are they here? Why are they not joyful?"

"I cannot answer your questions, Jade," her mother said. "This is your journey, only you can see them. Remember why you are here."

"Dad, I'm looking for my dad."

"Then, ask them, Jade," her mother said. "Ask them if they know where he is. You're seeing them for a reason."

"How?"

"With your heart. Connect with the water, Jade," Kevin said, taking off his jacket.

Jade waved away his offer of the jacket as she looked into the darkness of the water. If only it was daylight, it wouldn't seem so scary. Resisting the urge to shed tears on behalf of the spirits, she let her bag drop to the ground and walked into the cold water that flowed down from the mountain.

"Jade, what are doing? You'll catch your death," her mom called.

What a strange comment, Jade thought, as her whole body dropped under the water. She stretched her legs, searching for the bottom with her feet. A long, slimy eel brushed by her, its undulating body leaving illuminated streams of water in its wake. Great Turtle had taught her to swim and to not fear the water or the creatures below. Many times together, they had swum underwater with the giant sea turtles. The record for holding her breath had been for three minutes and eight seconds.

Jade looked into the depths of the dark water and saw a red glow. She dived down toward it. The deeper she went, the darker it became, and the brighter the light grew. It was coming from an underwater cave. She swam into the cave and surfaced quietly into a chamber of cold, smoky air; she stifled a cough. Shadows flickered on the limestone walls. It was no larger than the size of a basketball court.

As a fire burned, the smoke trailed up to the ceiling. Around a campfire sat five men dressed in traditional Native American clothing. Drumming and chanting, they appeared to be in a trance. She felt like an intruder.

Ripples of water expanded away from her body to lap at the rocky ledge. Her nose barely above the water, she was careful not to alert them to her presence as she moved toward the edge. Every bone in her body was telling her to dive back under and get out, but she had to know if they knew anything about her father.

She shifted away from the men into the shadows. Slowly, conscious of every sound she made, she hauled her body up onto land. She paused as the water trailed away from her clothes, splashing back into the pool. Each drip sounded like large, heavy raindrops. Perched on the rock, she waited for a few seconds before she clambered over a few smaller boulders. The chanting stopped. Jade sat still, rounding her shoulders, mimicking the rock.

"Raven Wings, your fear is like the rabbit, but you're courageous like the mountain lion and gentle as the deer. Come and accept your destiny. We have been waiting."

4

Jade kept still. How did they know her name? Did *everyone* know her spiritual name? The drummer was drumming at a steady pace, the tempo beckoning her forward. The sound echoed off the limestone walls and four of the five men stood in the formation of a compass with their faces heavily painted. The elder wore a beaded head-band, the beads sewn in wavy lines with a blue, red, and white circle in the middle. The band covered his forehead, and a central strip of beads extended down to the center of his nose. The circle was a hypnotic third eye.

Her senses were heightened. The reptilian part of her brain had triggered mixed signals; she wanted to run, but was transfixed. How would she get back? She had entered the cavern on the left side, approximately five feet from where she had surfaced. It was highly probable that without a guiding light, she would drown before reaching the surface of the river. She couldn't take that chance. She needed to find an alternative way out.

"I'm looking for my father? He has dark hair, blue eyes, is a tad over six foot, and he was probably wearing loafers." She looked from one man to the next. Jade heard herself and thought she sounded stupid, speaking as if she was lost in a department store. "His name is Scott Freeman. People sometimes call him Professor."

The elder stood. His elongated shadow towered over her, casting her in darkness. His deep voice thundered. "Come, we have been waiting for you."

Jade wasn't so sure if they were real or ghosts. They looked solid enough, but she'd seen some strange things lately. She thought she should leave. Her mom and Kevin would be frantic; maybe even thinking she had drowned. She looked back at the mirror-like surface of the pool where the flames of the fire had taken on a life of their own, making the water look hostile. But she knew she had to stay to find out if these people could help her find her father.

"Tonight, you'll meet your destiny. Look at the walls and see your destiny." The elder extended his arms out. "Come."

She looked across the pool of water to the cave wall, but it was dark and smoky. There too many flickering shadows from the raging flames. Standing at the edge of the water, ready to dive back in, she heard the distant sound of someone calling her name. It sounded like her father. The voice was muffled as if it was coming from inside the walls.

"Dad?" she whispered. She curled her toes in her shoes, trying to grip the edge of the rock to stop herself falling into the water. The voice was flat, a little too deep, and the words a little too slow. She was unsure if it was him or not. She had to find out so she faced the men.

The man wearing the third eye on his head spoke abruptly. "Come, drink."

Jade took a few steps away from the edge and followed the eroded curves of the cave wall. The smoke was rising; it had to be going somewhere, so there was more than one way out. The rock surface was slippery. The men resumed their chanting. As she drew closer and closer, a shiver raced up and down her spine. She stopped outside the circle, and the man she thought was a shaman danced, counterclockwise, toward her. He reminded her of the prairie bird, the sharp-tailed grouse. He left the circle and went behind her which forced her to step into the circle, then the chanting ceased. The four men now sat down cross-legged on the dirt floor. Jade felt the heat of the fire and smelled the dampness of the ground. It seemed real.

"I just want to find my father and then I'll leave. I think I heard him calling me. Do you know him? Professor Scott Freeman."

The medicine man was blurred, his features hazy. He continued to dance in spirals, faster and faster. It was making her dizzy. The youngest man, who had a necklace of herbs, rose from the south position, holding a small wooden bowl. He tore a strip from what looked like a dried mushroom and plucked bits from the other dried herbs around his neck, then placed them all in the wooden bowl. With a stick from the fire, he ignited the herbs. Jade expected the smell to be familiar, something that Great Turtle had burned, or old Chief Thundercloud when he sat under the tree across the road from her house. It occurred to her that Chief Thundercloud was protecting her and her family. But then, if her dad went with him, why is he in trouble?

The herbs had a foul, unpleasant odor. The herb man, starting at her feet, blew the smoke over her body. She couldn't help but inhale it and then she coughed as it trailed deeper into her lungs.

"Do you know Chief Thundercloud?" she asked in between coughs.

They continued to ignore her questions. She was starting to think her decision to stay was a big mistake. She had to get the hell out of there. At her left, another man stood. He had a chiseled nose and wrinkled leathery skin, and he encouraged her to sit. She refused and tried to step out of the circle, but the dancing shaman changed his direction, like a bird homing in on its prey. Jade panted, afraid.

The man on her left side, with the chiseled nose, yanked her to the ground, while the drummer increased his drumming. She crossed her legs, faced the fire and pretended not to be alarmed. The shaman, with his arms outstretched, danced to the manic, accelerating rhythm of the drum. The bowl that had been offered to her on arrival was placed in her hands and another piece of the dried mushroom was plucked from the necklace and crushed into it. A tiny vial of essences was produced and seven drops were added to the mix. Jade felt cemented to the ground with dread. She knew she was going to have to take at least a sip in case a refusal was considered offensive. She could pretend. *Just a sip*, she told herself. Then she would stand up quickly, dive back into the water, find the underwater opening, and get the hell out of there.

The potion smelled of old rotten socks. It was pungent, worse than a science lab experiment. Her nose wrinkled and her mouth sealed tight at the thought of drinking it. Scared it was going to taste worse than it smelled, she couldn't bring herself to move the bowl up to her mouth. The herb man came forward and touched her elbows, moving her arms upward. Mechanically, her arms moved the bowl up to her lips as instructed. She searched for her voice of reason, but it drifted away with every sip.

"More!" he said. Jade hesitated. "More. You must finish, and then you can go."

For some reason, she doubted they were going to let her go. Jade moved onto her knees, ready to leap up and dive into the water. She placed her lips on the rim of the carved bowl and drank. It dripped down the sides of her mouth as the man with the chiseled nose maintained pressure on her elbows, keeping the bowl pressed to her lips, making sure she drank it all.

"Drink. He is waiting for you in the Dream Lodge."

Gulping down the distasteful potion, Jade called out to

Kevin with her mind. She tried to stand to dive into the water, but her head was too heavy for her neck. *Where is the Dream Lodge, and who is waiting?* She wanted to ask. She tried to talk, but her tongue was thick, heavy in her mouth. The flames looked like tiny dancing women, getting brighter and brighter, stretching up, and looming over her. She watched them go round and round the fire like sadistic, hypnotic belly dancers. Animals scurried out from the middle of the flames, and birds materialized, taking flight. Eagles soared, a murder of crows, a bluish raven rose and cried out as if in pain. She dropped the bowl in her lap, then it toppled to the floor. How curious, she thought, and wanted to giggle. The smoke looked sinister. Her eyes felt like lead and her head lolled around. She was afraid her neck would snap as she fell backward, her upper body hitting the ground hard and driving the air from her lungs.

She struggled for air. The drumming resonated painfully throughout her body as if the drummer was pounding on her very bones. Her arms were pulled above her head and her legs were stretched out in front of her with her torso lifted off the ground. She was stretched as if she was on a medieval rack. Jade struggled, trying to free herself, but her efforts were ineffectual. She had been drugged and her mouth was dry. She choked on her breath, and coughed uncontrollably. Exhausted, she lay breathing heavily while someone removed her shoes. She could feel the heat from the fire. Her arms were outstretched and warm rocks, or maybe they were crystals, were placed in her hands along with on her stomach. The last one was placed on her fore-head and it was icy-cold. Jade felt terror. She had made a mistake and wanted to go home. Her ability to move her body was minimal. She tried to toss and thrash her body around, but it wouldn't budge. She was paralyzed which reminded her of the night terrors she had when she was younger. She tried to relax. The stones were warm, therapeutic. Jade tried to fall into herself to escape her growing fear, but the continual pounding of the drum compounded her sense of danger. Her eyelids fluttered, but she used her strength of will to open them, only to see that all the men were out of focus and distant. The shaman was hovering over her with his face painted blood-red. She decided she didn't want to see what was going to happen next. Just as she closed her eyes, a bear appeared in the flames. It reached out its paw to her, but she couldn't move. She couldn't get up and leave. Jade remembered what Noah had said: *The power of the bear is your strength.* She needed to go within herself to the womb-cave to align with the energy of Mother Earth and find solutions in the Great Void. Maybe then she would know how to return to Kevin and find her father.

In her mind, Jade took the paw and embraced the power of the medicine of the bear.

She sank down, through herself and even through the ground.

Images of people, in darkness, surrounded by glowing light, flashed behind her eyes. They were looking down on her, giving her the sensation of being at the bottom of a pit.

She wanted to shake the fear, but it rose from her stomach. Upon her dry tongue was the taste of dirt, and the stagnant smell of a well with damp walls filled her nose. Jade strained to maintain consciousness, willing herself to sit up, but it was useless. A heavy weight, a dark force, was pressing down on her chest... the shaman. She could still hear the beating of the drum and the walls of the well began to turn. Jade closed her eyes and her head spun. Faster and faster the walls rotated, until the floor and the walls were a whirlpool of energy. She stretched out her arms, trying to stop the spinning and she let out a bloodcurdling scream as she dropped into obscurity, tumbling into nothingness. As her body accelerated, she desperately tried to stop herself from flipping over and over, to take some control, but she had no form, no feeling of mass. There was nothing to see or hear. There was nothing. The acceleration and tumbling came to an abrupt end and she hung motionless in the infinite darkness.

A red dot appeared on a distant horizon. It pulsed, possibly indicating a distant tunnel up ahead. *It could lead back to the campfire in the cave,* she thought. She looked around for the bear, but all she could see was the expanding light. Hopeful that it might be the way out she tried to force herself into action. The red light was moving toward her and she strained to see. She could just make out the shape of a person at the center of the red light. *Kevin,* she cried. The light kept growing broader and taller, getting closer. Speeding toward her, the person's movements were jerky and erratic as they came closer. It wasn't Kevin. It was the shaman dancing toward her. He made a sharp turn in the opposite direction before he flickered and vanished. He reappeared in her peripheral vision, spiraling closer, then disappeared and again reappeared in front of her, closer still. Jade looked down at her feet, willing them to move. She saw nothing but infinity. He spiraled through space in the blink of an eye until he was mere yards away. His body spasmed and flashed, flickering in and out of focus, like a bad hologram projection as he kept coming.

He was two feet away; then a foot away and she could see a fox wrapped around his neck. The ginger fox smiled broadly like the Cheshire cat. The shaman reached out toward her stomach and scooped something from her solar plexus. She could feel a pull, like a hundred tentacles burrowed inside her and were now stuck trying to pull her inside out. Unable to tear her eyes away from the hypnotic ginger fox, the shaman's tentacle-like fingers slithered out from inside her and his cupped hands glittered like starlight. He raised his hands to his mouth and sucked in her shining light. As he grew in stature, he pulsed with color and vapors wafted from his body.

She was weakening, her mind cloudy. Panicked, Jade looked away, trusting it was all a bad dream. She looked down and saw her heart glowed with a brilliant pink and white energy. He reached out again and pushed his hand into her chest and she recoiled as if punched. She felt his hand plunge through her skin into her being. His head tilted back in bliss, depleting her power. She had to act. She had to move. Her mind was sluggish, but she envisioned gripping his wrist with her hands and pulling his hand from her body.

Faces flashed in her mind, interrupting her focus; they tried to speak with her. Some of the faces were riddled with fear, screaming in pain, trying to escape a demon with slippery skin. It had rows of pointed yellow teeth in a mouth too big for its face, which looked like a melting candle; its eyes were orange. Despair began to enter her heart and thoughts. Who was she kidding? She was never going to find her father. She was useless. Jade felt sad, confused, and cringed from the terror-filled faces yelling at her. She wanted to curl up in a ball and die. She couldn't think straight. Her mind was fragmenting. She smelled the bear from the woods and asked, *where is my father and how do I get out of here?*

The voice of her father whispered in her ear. "You must leave. You are in the void of nothingness, between two realms. Don't try to find me. Promise me you will never return."

The voice was labored, but she was sure it was his. She could hear the kindness, the love, and the struggle in each word.

"You have to fight the Shaman," he said. "Leave this place, or you will die. He wants the morning star, he wants your light. He wants your soul, and he will kill you for it. I'm here. But I am not. Go back, Jade, and forget me." His words drifted away.

"Dad, wait! Take me with you, don't leave me here alone."

"Wake up!" she heard. It was very faint. She thought

about it as if the meaning was foreign to her. The sensation of a hand wrapping around her heart returned.

"Jade, wake up," she heard. The words were no more than a whisper. She thought she was imagining it, going crazy like Noah had warned. She could come back as mad as a hatter.

The shaman squeezed and Jade cried out in pain. "Stop! Please stop!" She was begging him to stop when an explosive force of golden light crashed into him, fragmenting everything on impact. He was launched into the infinite blackness.

Jade bent over, clutching her chest, expecting her heart to be gone. She was ready for her hands to touch an empty cavity. Golden light swirled around her and sparkling atoms stuck to her invisible body, giving it form and strength, reminding her of how the little fish swam with the turtles, cleaning them. She could feel her chest, arms and legs bathed in the golden essence as her great-grandmother stepped from the light and embraced her. Jade's heart overflowed with love and light.

"You must go, feel for Mother Earth beneath you," Great Turtle said stepping aside to reveal Kevin shimmering in the distance at the end of a sparkling golden carpet.

"I have so many questions," Jade said.

"Jade, wake up!" She heard Kevin in her head and saw his urgent wave in the distance.

"Quickly, we must go," he said.

"Leave Raven Wings, we will meet again. Listen to your heart, not so much your head." Great Turtle vanished as quickly as she had arrived.

The heaviness of her body pressing against the cold cave floor filtered into her awareness. The musty smell of dampness filled her nostrils and her cheek stung. A slap! Her eyes fluttered open.

"Wake up, damn it," Kevin said.

Her eyes widened and fixed on his hand, which was drawn back for a third slap, but he let it drop.

No longer did she feel the fire at her feet. There was no campfire. There were no men. They were alone. Kevin's torch made a small portion of the cave visible, while the rest was cloaked in darkness. They were completely alone.

"Jade! Are you okay?" Kevin looked concerned. He tucked a strand of her hair behind her ear. The electricity between them was stronger. He pulled her into a sitting position, tucked her head under his chin, and wrapped his arms around her. He was strong and she felt safe, so he held her until she stopped shaking.

She tilted her head up. "Where did they go? "My dad spoke to me." Jade wanted to tuck her head back under Kevin's chin and let him hold her forever. She was so tired. "Will you help me find him?"

Kevin cradled her face in his hands, pausing before reaching her lips. He looked deep into her eyes, his brow and nose resting against hers, and he whispered, "I heard you calling me. I dived into the water and followed a beacon of light that led me here. The cave was dark when I surfaced. I waved my torch around, and saw you lying here, but you weren't alone."

Jade's body stiffened. "You saw them!"

"Don't make any sudden moves. I saw mysterious shapes rushing from your body, and like chameleons, they've blended into the walls. One didn't flee straightaway; he was like a devil sucking the life from you. His face was buried in your chest."

Jade listened intently and could feel eyes watching them. She felt violated. She pushed hard on Kevin's brow with hers and held onto him, wanting to hide in his aura.

"I crept out of the water and lunged at him. He exploded into a million pieces," Kevin said. "He turned to dust. But not for a minute am I going to assume he has gone. We have to get out of here."

Kevin pulled away and handed Jade her shoes. Quickly, she tied her shoelaces.

She couldn't stop shaking, but stood with Kevin's help. She leaned slightly against him, and could feel the warmth of his body fill hers, but she still shivered.

Kevin took in deep breaths, as he readied himself for the underwater swim.

"Who were they, Kevin?"

"I don't know. Maybe a jealous shaman. They must have lured you here for your power. We've got to get out of here. You ready?"

"I don't have any power." Jade touched her chest and recalled the violation of a hand squeezing her heart.

"Well, someone obviously thinks you do." Kevin walked to the edge of the water. He shoved the torch into the pocket of his pants and held out his hand to Jade. "You coming?"

Her muscles were too relaxed, her legs were like jelly. She didn't know if she could make the swim back, but she took his hand anyway.

"Stay close," he said as he clutched her hand tighter.

Together they drew in a few deep, breaths, filling up the lower part of their lungs, and jumped into the cold water.

The entrance to the cave was a little further then she expected, but once through to the other side, she saw streams of moonlight penetrating the depths. Kevin was a strong swimmer and kept a firm hold of her hand. Her oxygen was diminishing; the need to breathe was becoming urgent. Then she broke the surface of the still water, gulped and swallowed air.

"Jade," Kevin said.

He drew her close. She could feel her heart racing and was grateful she still had one. He bent his head backward into the water, so his hair streamed away from his face. She thought again how handsome he was as he wiped the dripping water off his forehead before shifting a strand of her hair that lay across her mouth.

"Are you okay?" he asked, searching her face.

She was still trying to catch her breath and tread water. She leaned in and lightly rested her hands upon his shoulders.

"My muscles were like jelly," she said.

"You did good Jade." Kevin drew her into an embrace,

holding them both up.

She could feel her body pressing against his and wrapped her arms around his neck. It felt good to melt into him and it would be easy to lose herself that way. Steady in his arms, she gazed over his shoulder. He pulled his head and chest slightly back, forcing her to look at him. His lips gently brushed hers, warm and soft. His heart was pounding against her chest, but before their lips pressed firmly together, Jade heard their names breaking the magic. Her mother was calling, searching for them.

"Jade! Kevin! Where are you? Jade, can you hear me? Kevin, where are you?"

Her mom stood in the water up to her chest as she waved her torch.

"She can't swim. The riverbed could drop suddenly." Jade pushed out of Kevin's arms and started to swim.

"Go back, Mom," she cried out. Jade dropped her face into the water and swam as fast as she could.

"Jade!"

Jade reached her mom and threw her arms around her. "I thought I lost you. I thought I lost you both."

She hugged Jade fiercely. "Thank you, Kevin."

Jade coughed as she walked from the river. Her mother immediately rummaged through the bag and fished out Jade's inhaler and Jade inhaled deeply.

"Let's go home this is too dangerous and you need spiritual protection," her mom said.

"No. There's no going back," Jade assured.

5

J ade sat on the bank shivering, confused and shaken. She wrapped her arms around herself, trying to catch her breath and sort out her thoughts. She was tired and didn't know what to do, or where to go. *What the hell was that all about? Who were those men and why did they attack me?*

"What happened?" her mother asked while she added wood to the fire she built.

"I was led to an underwater cavern where I saw a men's ceremony being performed. I thought I was intruding, but they said they were waiting for me. They summoned me. I am so gullible because I thought they knew where dad was, but I think they just wanted to destroy me. I drank a potion... they drugged me."

At that, her mom came over to check her pupils were normal. "Let's get you dry," she said, concerned.

Kevin said, "I'm going to head back to your place, and get you some dry clothes. It will take me ten minutes tops. I can see an image of your kitchen clearly in my head so it won't take me long."

"I don't want you rummaging around in my drawers," Jade said.

"And this is my favorite t-shirt. If I'm going to be successful finding dad, I need to wear this shirt."

"That makes no sense, Jade," her mom said.

"I know. But none of this makes sense. I'm trying something different. I visualized I was victorious and we were all back at the campground, hugging, and I'm wearing these clothes. I can't change them."

"I didn't know you were superstitious," Kevin said with a grin.

"I'm not. It's just what I envisioned I would be wearing after I found my dad. I don't know what will happen in between, but I have to hold on to the image and the feelings so it will come true," Jade said.

"Where did you hear that?" her mom asked.

"Tim said that's what you do, K." She could see in the firelight that Kevin was blushing.

"Anyway, Jade, take your shirt off and wear my windbreaker until your shirt's dry." Kevin turned and faced the fire while she did. He also took off his own shirt, exposing the muscles in his back and his narrow waist to her view.

"I'll get some sticks to hang your clothes from," her mom said, going back into the forest.

The smell of Kevin lingered in the jacket and she hugged it close to her.

"I saw Great Turtle," Kevin said. "She guided me to you and she hid me from the shaman stealing your power. She reminded me of my grandmother."

"I saw her too," Jade said. "It was good to see her."

Jade's mom walked out of the forest with an armload of wood. Kevin rushed to help her. "No, you get back in front of that fire and dry off those pants, or you will catch your death and your mother will have my hide."

Kevin smiled and winced.

"You'd better stand at the fire and rotate," Jade said, and knew his mom would be devastated if anything happened to him.

"I don't know why you insist on staying here when we can simply go back home through the portal and get you some dry clothes." Her mom dropped the wood by the fire and hung their clothes to dry. "It's nice Great Turtle is watching over you, Jade. I miss her."

Jade wished she could communicate with Great Turtle at will. Maybe Sophia or Casey could teach her, but now wasn't the time to head back ... she'd been going to say "home", which surprised her. She was started to think of the others as her family. Being an only child had its benefits, but she had to admit it was kind of nice having other girls around, especially Rachel.

"I also heard Dad. He sounded strained, helpless and in pain. If we leave, I may lose the connection."

Her mom stopped what she was doing and turned around, scanning the area.

Jade looked behind herself self-consciously to see what her mom was searching for.

"Is he still with you?" her mom said.

It broke Jade's heart that her mom continually searched for him. "No." Jade struggled to hold back the tears. Her intelligence hadn't prepared her for the spiritual world. The spiritual world was something she had once mocked; she sided with science and skepticism, but seeing what Kevin, Sophia, and Casey could do made her feel ashamed.

Jade thought her great-grandmother just happened to know how to use plants and the environment to her benefit. She listened to her explain the different medicinal benefits of plants, and why people came to her. Great Turtle could've earned a degree in herbal medicine, become a surgeon— anything. Instead, she became the healer. Jade had always felt Great Turtle could have aspired to be more. Now, under-standing how ignorant she was, made her feel sick andnaive. There were so many energy fields, and so many possibilities — she never previously considered other realities. "Great Turtle, I'm so, so sorry. I have been a fool, and I am now in dire need of your wisdom."

"Who are you talking to?" Kevin asked.

Jade's eyes darted from side to side, surprised she had said that out loud. "Great Turtle."

"Did she answer you?"

"No, she didn't. I don't understand the world of the spirit,

K, and that makes this journey extremely dangerous. I'm liable to get us all trapped in some unknown realm with my father. Or killed. Maybe you and my mom should go back home. The world has changed. It's not the same as before and I don't think it's a utopian world. I think the space around Casey's estate might be the only utopian place there is, and the rest of the Earth might be..."

"Be what ...?"

"I don't know," Jade said, shaking her head in confusion. "My head hurts from thinking. I can't recall feeling like this before."

"I'm not going anywhere, Jade. We're in this together. I've noticed something's wrong, too. It's like the rules of what's real in the world and what's an illusion has changed. If you want, I can take your mom back though." He sat down beside her.

Jade felt the warmth radiating from his leg. In close proximity to Kevin, she always felt a spark of electricity, like their atoms were splicing and joining together.

"Will you two stop talking like I'm not here," her mom said, stoking the fire. "If you think I might jeopardize the safety of you and your father, I'll return to the lake and wait at the cabins for you. Otherwise, I'm going all the way. I want to find your father. He's the love of my life and I've missed him for two years. I cannot stand to be away from him any longer. It pains me that he hasn't called out to me, so stop acting like I'm not important."

"Maybe it's because he doesn't know you're alive and I

was the last person he talked to," Jade said. "We should have left sooner to find him."

"We couldn't," Kevin said. "You know that. Sophia said it wasn't safe because the world hadn't finished unfolding."

"But did we have to wait for five months?" Jade's mom said angrily.

"Mrs. Freeman, I tried, and there was nothing beyond the walls of Athanasia."

"Maybe you were just frightened!" her mother said.

Kevin flinched from her words. "It had nothing to do with me. I created the doorways, and we went nowhere but into the next room."

Jade knew it had everything to do with his fear of others getting hurt, as well as the unknown. He had told her and the others the night before they left.

"Mom! It's not Kevin's fault that we had to wait for the world to catch up. And, quite frankly, I don't think it has yet," Jade said.

Her mom stared hard at her, a massive frown creasing her forehead. "Guys, you're both glowing with energy." She tried to step forward, then recoiled slightly, like she had bumped into a force field. "I've never seen anything like it before."

Kevin pulled his leg away from Jade's. She hadn't realized they were still touching, but her cargos were warm and her whole body was heating up. She could see the steam coming off the leg of her pants, and Kevin's too. A light buzz filled her being.

"Can you feel that?" Kevin said, looking at Jade. He

seemed to want to smile, excited at what was happening, but wasn't sure if it was okay.

Jade turned toward Kevin, noticing that his wet hair was nearly dry. He pushed his fringe off his face, revealing soft eyes filled with wonder.

"As soon as you moved your leg, Kevin, the light dimmed and disappeared. Are you doing that? Or is it a result of you connecting with Jade," her mom asked.

"I see a resemblance," he said, half smiling at them both. "And I don't know." He shifted uncomfortably.

"Out of curiosity, put your hand on her leg." Kevin did. There was no visible light, or any sparks. But Jade could feel her tummy fluttering, and she knew Kevin could feel it too.

"Jade, can you feel anything," her mom asked.

"No. How about you, K?" said Jade, hoping he would go along with her.

Kevin disengaged from Jade and got up off the log, walking closer to the fire. He cleared his throat. "No, nothing."

"Oh. Well, the glow has faded. Maybe we should try and get some sleep," her mom said.

"I don't think I can close my eyes. I'll keep watch," Jade responded, taking out her notebook. "You two go ahead and get some sleep."

Jade drew the image of the shaman, and the herbs pictured on the necklace the youngest man had worn. Her hand was sore as she scribbled down the details of her experience in between realms.

Jade gazed over at her mom, who was sleeping peacefully by the fire. Quietly, she unzipped the backpack and slipped in her notebook. She edged closer to a wide awake Kevin and whispered, "There are so many things I don't understand: apparitions, ghosts, talismans. And the world seems, in one moment, to have no life, and then it does, and then it doesn't. As if time is stopping and starting. I don't know what occurred when we closed the gate to the underworld but –" said Jade.

"What do you mean by talismans? Do you mean totems, like Noah and Charlie spoke of? I can feel the atmosphere shift. I can feel life emerging," Kevin said.

"My bracelet, Sophia's necklace, their talisman. Yeah, but I was thinking more about totems, animals. This is all so strange, but it shouldn't be. Great Turtle tried to share her magical world with me, but I just didn't believe." She picked up a few sticks and tossed them into the fire. Her shirt was dry. She checked Kevin's, and it was dry too. Reluctantly, she threw it to him. "We should get some rest." A part of Jade believed the bear was watching and waiting for her, but she'd had enough of intuition for one day. Jade ignored the calling of the bear, kept her eyes wide open, and waited for the sun to rise.

WAITING FOR THE RISING OF THE SUN DRAGGED OUT THE silence between them. Jade, unable to sleep, stared into the fire, replaying what had happened in the cavern. The concoction she had been given, at first had forced her into a similar state as the one her mother had eased into her when they'd entered the woods. She had been alone, deep within herself. The concoction had paralyzed her, pushed her out of her body and she had sunk into the ground; a vast endless area, and a different space and time. Maybe even a different realm. It was impossible... all objects had vanished and she had been suspended. It was darkness—a place of separation, sorrow, despair, and death. Perhaps it was *truly* a different realm. If Great Turtle, her father, and Kevin hadn't come, would death in the timeless world of despair have been her future? It wasn't a place she ever wanted to go back to.

"Mom?' Her mother laid on the ground and looked like she might be sleeping.

"Hmm?"

Jade's hand moved up to her face and pushed back her phantom glasses. Even though her eyesight had been 20/20 since being in Athanasia, she still acted as if she wore glasses. She also found herself squinting to see distance, when it was really perfectly clear. She pulled her now-dry ponytail over her shoulder and began running her fingers through the knots. "Can you teach me to go into that state; the one when we first entered the woods?"

Her mother slowly sat up, pulled her arms behind her back, and stretched. "Do you understand what happens to you internally, and how you affected your external surroundings?"

"You calmed me down so I wouldn't have an asthma attack," Jade said. "I go within and relax my breathing."

"No. Well, yes, but that's not all it is. And you need to ask yourself, why are you getting asthma attacks when you've been healed of all your ailments?"

"Can you teach me, or not?" Jade asked. Kevin opened his eyes and folded his arms.

"What?" Jade said, with a condescending look. "Why are you getting your back up?" Kevin said.

"Why do you speak in riddles?" Jade said, flinging her hair back over her shoulders. "Mom, are you going to teach me?"

"There is not much I can teach you. You have the knowledge within you. Do you remember the stories of the stones? Once you do, you will have your answers."

"Oh god, now *you're* talking in riddles."

"How's that a riddle?" Kevin asked, standing up and dusting leaves off his clothes.

"What stones, Mom?"

"There are seven stones with drawings on them, and each one tells a story that belongs to you. Great Turtle taught you these stories as songs to help you with your gifts. When Great Turtle died, you stopped singing the songs. Your dad and I wanted you to stop. I tried to find the stones among her things, but they were gone. They weren't happy songs, Jade."

"What are you talking about? You know what, forget I asked!" Jade said, irritated, and she walked away down to the river. She watched the movement of the water. *Was it always this calm,* she wondered? Jade rummaged through her mind for the memory of the stones and came up blank. Kevin must have stood up to follow, because Jade heard her mother telling him to leave her be.

The dawn light was yet to break over the treetops. Her mom was right. Why was she still having asthma attacks? Was fear causing the constriction of her airways? She'd laughed when she'd heard of terror vomiting, when someone saw something terrifying and they would just puke their guts up. And what did her mom mean by how she affected her external surroundings? Kevin had asked her how she made the forest breathe.

Jade watched the twinkling light of the sun just below the horizon and wished it would hurry up. It sparkled on the water as if an hour had passed. Jade could see the bear rising, standing up on his hind legs and giving out a bellowing yawn. She turned back and saw Kevin urinating on the fire, but her mother was walking toward her. "I was wondering how long it would take you," she said.

Jade was puzzled by her words. "To do what?"

She put her arm around her daughter's shoulders and said, "It's a beautiful morning, Jade. What's even more beautiful, is you."

"Thanks. Sorry, I was angry," Jade said. "Why is Kevin urinating on the fire?"

"I asked him to put it out. He said he had to go, and he could kill two birds with one stone." She chuckled.

Jade turned to see Kevin kicking dirt onto the fire before picking up their backpacks.

"Drink?" asked her mom, offering Jade the nozzle to the hydration pack that was slung over her shoulder.

"Sure, why not."

JADE TOOK THE LEAD AND HEADED TOWARD THE PLACE THE bear had slept. She was surprised at how comfortable she was becoming around nature. At one time it would have totally freaked her out; she would have thought the bear would attack them. Now, in her heart, she knew it wanted to help.

"Do you have a plan?" Kevin asked, walking beside her.

"We'll keep following the river. All I know is I have to go southeast. Did you see the deer last night?"

"When?" Kevin kept his head down, watching his feet as he walked. His fringe dropped over the side of his face, hiding his eyes from her.

"In the fog," said Jade.

"I didn't see anything." He reached up to loop his thumbs under the backpack's straps. "How did you speed up time?" he asked.

Sometimes Kevin comes up with the strangest notions and ideas, thought Jade. *He is handsome, cute, and surprisingly very emotionally intelligent, but he still... he still what? He always* asks curious questions. Jade was on the verge of understanding something. A thought was running around in her mind that she couldn't catch. It was like looking into a room, knowing all the items there and where they all belonged, but you also know there's something different. She felt like that now. What was different wasn't a tangible item, it was metaphysical, foreign. *Focus on Dad; find him, and you'll find the answers.*

She slipped on a rock.

Kevin caught her arm. "Are you alright?" Her skin tingled. "I'm good."

The bear came into view as the river narrowed. It left the shoreline, heading into the woods. Jade stopped and wondered if she should follow the creature.

"What's wrong?" her mom asked. "You have to go back."

"I'm not leaving, Jade. We'll find your dad together." "I don't want you to get hurt, Mom."

"When I'm with you, nothing can hurt me."

"I'm going to follow that bear, Mom. It could turn and kill any one of us." She spoke, but doubt filled her words.

Kevin pushed his hair back off his face and moved awkwardly. "What bear?"

"The bear we've been following for the past hour!" Jade huffed, holding a stance with her hands on hips, she stuck her neck forward. Her brow knitted in astonishment. "Seriously! You didn't see the bear that just entered the woods? Mom, you saw it, right?"

"No bear, Jade."

"K, come on, you saw it. Is this a joke? We don't have time

for jokes." She stormed off in the direction of the bear and called out over her shoulder. "If you don't leave for your own safety, Mom, then you'd better keep up." Jade yelled as she ran into the woods, leaving them both behind.

THE FOREST WAS EERILY QUIET, NOT EVEN A RASPY CHIRP FROM a hungry baby bird could be heard, or the flap of a wing. She expected at least one bird to take flight as she stumbled through the forest after the bear. The trees loomed over her. No winds passed and there were no smells, either sweet or sour. It was like the world was frozen, again. She pressed her feet into the leaves on the floor of the forest—silence. Impossible! She spun around. Her mother and Kevin were nowhere to be seen. Jade crept forward, afraid to breathe, and an overwhelming sensation of the need to cough pushed against her chest. She worried that if she let the cough out, she would alert some unknown force to her location, so she thought better of it.

Jade stood perfectly still. The scent of blueberries was upon her breath and the taste on her tongue made her mouth water. A feather, soft and light, dragged across her face, bringing the shaman into sight. He emerged from the tree she was standing in front of, but she didn't know if he could see her, so she kept very still. The scent of decay surrounded him. The other tribesmen stepped from the camouflage of the trees inches away from her where they had been hiding. She hoped to god Kevin and her mom would stay by the river. She watched the men moving away, heading further into the woods, sniffing the air like animals aware of an unseen presence. Jade needed to exhale. Desperate to breathe, she imagined them moving faster as they cautiously searched the brush. As soon as it was safe, she let out a sigh. Perplexed, she stayed where she was. How had she remained undetected? She held her hands up to her face; they looked normal. She wasn't translucent, and she wasn't dead—was she? Or maybe we're all dead—ghosts? Her hands seemed so solid. Jade recalled the spirits they had seen at Casey's when the veil between the worlds was thin, before they returned the Emerald Tablet; and the way New York had come alive with color after the implosion. The ghostly figures had solidified, allowing Jade to see there were so many layers to this new post-apocalyptic world.

Her eyes closed, she slowed her breathing, and imagined the feeling of the wind. She breathed out any confusion and breathed in clarity. As she breathed in, she imagined it was afternoon; the birds were chirping, searching for food, and her mother and Kevin were by her side. The depths of her mind were vast, and she could feel herself moving. It was if she was rising upward, swimming through water.

"Jade?" Her mom called out her name. "Jade! You're doing it, Jade."

It was too much for her to fully comprehend, but she had a good idea of what it was she was doing. It was totally impossible, but it was happening. If she was right, it would be afternoon; Kevin, who she could already smell, would be next to her, and the birds that she could hear would be chirping. Before she opened her eyes, Kevin spoke.

"Before you come back, imagine a door and lock it. Lock the door that opens to the other realms. Don't leave yourself open."

Jade focused on Kevin's words and imagined a purple, translucent door frame that had golden edges, and a heavy medieval door, its metal reinforcements tarnished green. She placed a golden star, the Seal of Solomon, on the door, just like the one in her paintings with the green gate. Once it looked right, she backed away from the door and the vastness, remembering the present, the woods, the birds, the wind, her mother and Kevin's voice.

Her head was tilted to the sky. She listened to the clear sounds around her. *I did that, but how?* She wondered.

"It's impossible. Mom, how is this possible." Jade waited for a scientific reason; her eyes pleading for one as she searched her mom's face.

Her mother shook her head. "I don't know. When you were little, Great Turtle and I would joke around and ask you for a weather report because you mimicked the weather reporter on television, and it was funny. But, then it stopped being funny when you were right eighty percent of the time. Sun, rain, wind, hurricanes—you name it, you predicted it. Great Turtle thought it was marvelous, but I eventually made her promise not to ask you again. I was afraid it was the beginning of something bigger. Like this. You can do more than predict the weather. You can change it if you go within yourself to what Great Turtle called the womb-cave of the Dream Lodge. Right now, you are sensing and doing much more than predicting or changing the weather. You just accelerated time." Her mom tried to read Jade's face.

"I didn't accelerate time, and I don't remember anything about weather reports," Jade said.

"We stopped when you were about six," her mom offered.

"It feels like everything branches out in different directions; nothing is linear or finite any more. Everything now has infinite possibilities. Why didn't you mention this before?"

"We thought it had stopped. Great Turtle was taking care of you while your dad and I worked. Slowly, we forgot about it."

"Is there anything else about me you've forgotten?" Jade asked with a sarcastic tone.

"Jade, really!" said Kevin as he moved uneasily. "You're frightened, confused, excited, feeling totally unbalanced by everything that is happening. You feel foolish, regretful ..."

"Okay!" Jade said. "Stop reading my emotions."

"Don't attack your mom. She wants to find your dad just as much as we all do. She misses him too, you know. He's her best friend, and she's afraid it may already be too late."

"Okay, Kevin, that's enough," her mom said. Her eyes were moist. She took the nozzle of her water pack and placed it in her mouth, but didn't bite down.

"Mom, I'm so insensitive. We'll find him; I know we will." Jade touched her mom's shoulder and gently rubbed it.

"You're so much more than we know, Jade. This isn't a movie, this is the real you unfolding."

"Shh!" She had the feeling as if someone had just walked over her grave and it sent a shiver racing through her body. "The shaman and his warriors are close," Jade said, as she searched the trees around them. Trusting her inner voice, she pointed out and whispered to her mom and Kevin. "This way."

6

Keeping low and pausing behind random trees, Jade moved through the forest like a hunter. The forest was noisy to her desensitized ears and everything was now amplified. Her heartbeat, the rustling of leaves that made her picture opossums, rats, or raccoons scurrying around. The unnerving sound of a fox sounded like a woman's scream. Even worse were the snakes slithering down the trees, in and out of the underbrush, and heading in their direction. From the look on Kevin's face, he either heard them too, or was well aware of her fear-induced feelings.

Believing the snakes were pursuing them made Jade move even faster. She would be running if she thought her mother could keep up. An hour had passed since she last saw the river and they were heading into dense woods. She closed her eyes and filtered the sounds of the forest, searching for the flow of water cascading down from the mountain streams.

The cry of an eagle pierced Jade's ears. "Damn bird!" Afraid her ears would rupture, she clapped her hands over them, hunching over in the process. She squeezed her head tight, waiting for the intense cry to stop. Kevin crouched beside her and leaned into her face. He mouthed something, but she couldn't hear him. He touched her hands, trying to pull them away from her ears. Jade noticed that he didn't seem to be bothered by the noise, but to her, it was one long continuously agonizing screech. Then, suddenly, it stopped. Panting, she uncapped her ears slowly; the high frequency of the eagle's cry still reverberated in her head. Kevin helped her to her feet. The fragment of a song came to mind, something about from above I see all, be the observer, something, something, and fear not... she tried to remember the words, but couldn't.

"Are you okay?" her mom asked. "That was insane," Kevin said.

"Did you hear it too?" Jade said, rubbing her ears and jaw. She could tell from his pursed lips and half smile that he hadn't.

"No, but I felt your anguish. What was it? And what are we running from? What aren't you saying?" Kevin met her eyes, begging her to confide in him. "I feel it, Jade, but I just don't understand it. Give me something."

"The forest is loud. We're running from snakes, hundreds of slithering snakes. You didn't see them?"

Kevin frantically searched the ground around his feet, hopping from one foot to the other as if he was standing on hot coals. "Where?"

Her mom glanced over her shoulder and up into the trees. "Focus on the sounds of where you're going, not where you are," she said, turning back to Jade.

"I was trying to." Jade frowned.

"Then, try again. Focus. Where do you want to go?"

Jade wished she could see through the eyes of the eagle. She felt the air beneath its wings and the hawk-like gaze from high in the sky. More of that song was on the tip of her tongue as she took flight with the bird in her mind.

Kill the rabbit and swallow your fear,
On the wings of the eagle, rise beyond the trees,
Become the observer and see, see, see.
Listen to your heart and follow your soul,
It doesn't really matter if you're young or old,
As the observer, you will see, see, see.
So, kill the rabbit and swallow your fear ...

Through the eyes of the majestic eagle, as it glided on the currents of air, Jade could see the fresh sparkling waterfall that spilled over a cliff edge and splashed into a crystal clear pool below. High up on the wet, slippery rock face, hidden by the shadow of the cliff, were caves. Her father's body lay in one of those caves; she felt the pull in her solar plexus and just knew it to be true. Jade imagined the fresh tumbling water, the spray in the air, the clear blue sky, and the stones she would need to jump across, to then climb up to the caves and rescue her father. She was not a good climber and never excelled at any sports. Getting bouts of dizziness from vertigo put a dampener on a lot of activities, but if she could pick and choose when to see through the eyes of the eagle, it would make things easier. Jade opened her eyes and thanked the eagle in the sky. She looked into her mother's face for a second, before running in the direction of the waterfall.

"Wait!" Kevin called out.

"Take care of my mom," Jade yelled over her shoulder.

"No, Jade!" her mom yelled after her.

Jade could hear her mother's voice fading as she continued to run. "Kevin, go, follow her. I'll be alright. I'll meet you back at the campground. Go, she might need your help. Go!" Her mom's words seemed to have been cut off in mid-sentence. There were a few seconds when she thought that she was alone, then suddenly Kevin was beside her. He swooped and ducked the branches and together they were like two cross-country runners, battling for the lead. The tumbling water grew louder as they neared the waterfall.

"It's just up here, I can feel it. The air is moist. Can you feel it?" Jade said, panting.

"Yes. Yes, I can feel it. It's real. It's in this realm," Kevin said.

"Do you mean to say that everything I have been seeing is from a different realm?" Jade asked with disbelief.

Kevin swallowed, trying to talk. He was having trouble

catching his breath, "Yep! We may have returned the Emerald Tablet and closed the gate to the underworld, but I don't think the prior damage was fully rectified. I think a lot of realms are clashing." His words were starting to make sense, causing Jade to stop. With her hands on her knees, she tried to catch her breath. "That's what I was afraid of. Maybe *we* opened the doors to different realms."

"We didn't open the doors; when The Emerald Tablet was removed for the tomb of Thoth the doors to dark realms were unlocked and slowly opened by what was on the other side. I believe whatever ventured from those realms are still here. Maybe we didn't return The Emerald Tablet in time," Kevin paused, before continuing. "Who are we to think we know the mind of God."

"But doesn't it say in the Bible, in the Book of Revelation, that there will be heaven on Earth or something? Would you call this heaven?" Jade said.

"I don't know. We'll have to talk to Sophia. She knows the scriptures," Kevin said.

"Can you hear that?" Jade looked hopeful, but was ready for him to say no.

"Did you ask the birds and insects to be quiet? I can't hear them. You're getting good at this, Jade. You're like the queen of wands." Seeing her perplexed facial expression, he tilted his head and concentrated. "I can hear the pounding waterfall." He suggested.

Their eyes met. "It's that way," he said, then ran off.

Within moments, they broke free of the dense forest and

saw a rocky embankment near a clear body of water. Lying on the rocks by the edge of the river, and floating on the water, were snakes—hundreds of snakes bathing in the sun, as if waiting for them to finally turn up.

There were species that didn't even exist in the region; species like Black mambas, king cobras, anacondas, and some were slithering. It was a kaleidoscope of color. It was that instant that Jade knew she would never again mock the notion of terror vomiting. The way the water moccasins were moving to the shoreline and piling up like boats moored in a harbor, copperheads and pygmy rattlesnakes were slithering over a six-foot black mamba and anaconda, she no longer thought it was amusing. She felt her stomach somersault.

"Tell me you do NOT see them, K." She didn't take her eyes off the snakes, hoping it was an illusion to scare her from trying to reach her father. "K!"

His little finger reached out and hooked around hers. "Hell, no!" he said. "What are they? Those ones coming out of the ground, and from around the rocks? This is bad."

"Eastern coral snakes," Jade said, afraid to move.

"Look, there are red-bellied blacks. Impossible, impossible!" Kevin turned to his side, checking for snakes.

"What are we going to do," Jade said, wiping her brow with her forearm. Across to her right, at the bottom of the waterfall, Jade watched the churning water as it hit the river below. We need to get up there. The easiest way would be climbing over those rocks against the rock wall, to scale up.

But the snakes are covering every inch of the embankment. We need to get up there to the top ledge, he pointed.

Kevin cleared his throat. "That's like fifty feet high. Let's move back. Maybe we can find another way up to the top of the cliff and then climb down."

"Climb down from up there. How? We'll need ropes." Taking a step back, keeping the snakes in view, she tried to hide behind some bushes.

"Maybe we could move closer to the ridge and slowly step over the ones at the edge. The ones that are butted up against the rocks, they don't seem as lively as those in the sun," Kevin suggested.

"Oh, no, you've got to be kidding me," Jade gasped.

"Come on, Jade, this way." Kevin took her hand. She walked back- ward, away from the snakes, terrified to take her eyes off them. "Breathe in calm, breathe out over-whelmed," she said.

"Overwhelmed! That's a bloody understatement," Kevin said.

Jade held Kevin's hand tighter as she turned cautiously, trying not to alert the snakes or any other predator that might be stalking them. It was hard to keep going. Her discomfort was increasing, and she was feeling like a coward. The sound of the waterfall was building. Kevin stopped and Jade crouched beside him to peer between the feather-like drooping leaves of a fern. The snakes weren't as plentiful in the shade, but there still wasn't more than a foot between them. She would have to walk on her tiptoes. Jade was uncoordinated at the best of times, but her vertigo symptoms had lessened since being in Athanasia. She felt the blood pounding in her head, liable to explode out of her ears if she didn't get herself under control. Okay... breathe in calm, breathe out stress; breathe in calm, breathe out fear; breath in calm, breathe out fear. She continued to repeat her mantra until she felt a bit more levelheaded and composed.

"We need a distraction," Kevin whispered. "Like a bar brawl that you see in the movies."

"So, all the snakes will run over and watch?" Jade, despite their dilemma, laughed at his ludicrous suggestion.

"Why are you laughing?"

"You've lost the plot. Okay, suppose it's possible. What sort of a distraction will entice those snakes to move so we can get past them?" Jade asked. Her knees were painful, pressing down on sharp twigs, so she had to stand.

"Actually, can you make the snakes go away? Like when you asked the birds to be quiet?" Kevin said, pulling her back down.

"I didn't ask the birds to be quiet. They just were. I don't know, K." Jade looked at him, doubtful. "I can try." Quickly she closed her eyes, but started to topple over. She opened her eyes and sat down properly. Adjusting her sitting position, she crossed her legs and concentrated on the awful images of the snakes in her mind until they were gone from the picture. Not leaving or slithering away into the forest or coming toward her, but just gone. The river shoreline in her mind cleared. Still and peaceful. "Is it working?"

Kevin was silent.

Peeking out through thin slits, she saw the snakes hadn't budged. They were still there, slithering over each other with no apparent change.

Kevin stepped from their hiding spot and took a step among the snakes; she saw they didn't move toward him.

"Kevin, get back here."

Jade covered her eyes in disbelief, and then pulled her hands away, praying she had been hallucinating. He took another step. The snakes appeared to be unfazed. On his right, toward the water's edge, two black mambas raised their heads and began to intertwine. Kevin kept very still.

"Come back!" Jade whispered.

Even though he looked petrified, he kept tiptoeing through the snakes. The snakes behind him stirred. Jade's eyes darted around, searching her mind for a solution. Fire! That would move them away, but how was she going to make a fire quick enough to save Kevin from a snake bite? A coral reef snake came up from the ground and slid onto the toes of K's shoe. It moved behind his ankle and up over his cargos and his calf muscle. She rifled the bush for his backpack, knowing he would have matches. Raising her eyes, she looked back at him and cringed because he was wearing his backpack.

Way back in the recess of her mind she heard Great Turtle asking her what was the weather going to be like today? Hot and sunny, or freezing cold? *Well, it's currently warm and sunny, but a northerly wind is going to bring a sudden change with freezing cold temperatures...*

Jade thought about a frozen lake, a snowplow, and frost on her breath. She wrapped her arms around herself to keep out the cold. Snow drifted from the sky, landing softly on her face. She opened her eyelids, crusted with ice, and saw the snow was real and to her relief, Kevin was shivering. The snake halfway up his leg was stiff, frozen solid. The snakes along the riverbank were covered by a layer of snow as well. She had to assume they were still there, just immobilized so she dug around in the brush and snow beside her for a thick fallen branch and ploughed her way to Kevin, pushing the snakes aside.

"Can you get Casey's knife out of my bag? Shaun slipped it into the front zipper pocket when he thought I wasn't watching," Kevin said. "That guy knows a hell of a lot more than he lets on."

"Use your bowie knife, K! I think Shaun gave it to you as a good luck charm. He really cares about you, cares about all of us. He just doesn't know how to show it. Do you think he'll come back?"

"Oh, right, my bowie knife," Kevin said, shivering. "How did you make it so cold, Jade? It's damn scary what you can do," Kevin said with an astonished look on his face.

"Yeah, it is," she replied.

Kevin concentrated on wedging the knife between his leg and the snake. "I think Shaun likes my mom and dad... I think my dad is the person he wished his dad had been."

Kevin winced as he accidentally scraped the blade against the skin of his leg, trying to get leverage.

"Why don't you take your shoe off, and then pull the snake down your leg?"

"That's too easy, Jade." Kevin smiled at her. His teeth were chattering. "Okay, let me lean on you."

His touch was warm upon her shoulder, even though he was shivering. She stepped in closer than she needed too and the sensation of energy from him the second he touched her, seemed endless and soothing. She drew in a deep calming breath, taking in his scent and she could feel her energy centers, from her head down to her groin, opening up as they merged into one. Time was distorted. Her eyes filled with color, like the aurora borealis over a mirrored lake. Had she stepped through the threshold of her inner iron gate? She didn't think so; it was more like she was within herself. The energy was her true expansive self, and her spirit was beautiful; she never would have thought herself as beautiful before. The image disappeared, and her eyes flew open. Kevin's nails, as he tried to balance on one foot, had dug into her shoulder as he searched her eyes with a look of wonder. He cleared his throat, smiled, and went back to putting on his shoe.

He took the branch from her and mimicked her previous actions to clear a pathway to the icy waterfall.

KEVIN CLIMBED UP THE FIRST TWO ROCKS AND SLIPPED ON THE ice. He steadied himself and reached a hand out to help Jade step across the same rocks. They were going to hoist themselves onto a ledge that was close to the cold stream of water cascading over the cliff edge above them, to get to the caves where her father lay. The spray was already turning into icicles.

As she placed her hands on the icy ledge to lever herself up, she felt as if they might stick to the rock. It was obviously too cold. They weren't going to be able to maintain their body heat for much longer and hypothermia could soon set in. She pulled her hands away carefully and rubbed them together, blowing her warm breath over them. Jade touched Kevin's face; his lips were turning blue. Everything around them was covered in snow. *What's happened to the birds?* Jade felt sad, and guilty about bringing on the next ice age. *Okay, that's a bit of an exaggeration,* she thought. *But how is it possible that I can make it snow? Well, if I did this, I can undo it. But if I heat the area up too quickly, will the tiny birds have a heart attack? And what about Kevin and me?*

"Jade, what is it?" Kevin said, breathing into his cupped hands. "I don't know if I can do this," she said.

"Yes you can, I know you can. It's really slippery, and cold, so be careful, I'm right here for you," he encouraged her. "At least I'm wearing my windbreaker. You don't have a jacket on."

"We won't be able to climb up without getting frostbite, probably.

And the birds; where have the birds gone. Did I kill them?"

"What ... the birds, no, I don't think so." Kevin glanced up into the sky. Not a bird in sight.

"See nothing; hear nothing," Jade said. "I have to undo this."

Kevin's eyes scanned the ground where the snakes lay under the layers of snow. "If you do, they will climb up after us. I was sure the snake on my leg had been about to take a chunk out of my ass."

"I'll try and create an autumn day, when the trees have changed, and it's cool, but not cold enough to freeze. If I don't, I think we will fall off the face of the cliff before we get to the caves." Jade latched onto Kevin to help lower herself down onto a rock covered in snow, and crossed her legs. She didn't want her legs dangling, just in case it became warm enough to stir the snakes.

She put her fingers under her armpits. *Okay*, she said to herself. *My fear is real, the snakes are real.* She controlled herself. She wanted the trees to breathe, and they did. What about the snakes? For some reason, she felt they were out of her jurisdiction, but the weather was apparently not. Jade took comfort in this revelation and began to imagine a lovely autumn day, and the way the sun felt on her face. The smell and colors of the deciduous trees as they changed; the maple leaves dancing in the wind. Autumn is a beautiful season and Jade vowed to appreciate the seasons of change so much more if they ever got back home.

"Jade! Jade, everything is changing. It's like one image is superimposed on top of the present, creating a new reality. Open your eyes and see the overlap. What is this? Maybe you shouldn't keep doing this until you understand what's happening." Kevin, with a gentle touch, nudged her knee. "We'd better keep moving." She opened her eyes and allowed him to pull her to her feet. Her chest brushed his, and Jade tried to take a step back, but slipped in a puddle of water from the melted ice. She fell toward him rather than away and he caught her against his chest, where she could feel his curves and the beating of his heart.

"We'd better go," he said. "Will you be okay pulling yourself up onto that ledge now, or do you want to use my knee as a step?" He relaxed his arms, letting her step away.

Catching her breath, she pushed her bracelet up her forearm, brushed a few stray strands of hair behind her ears and said, "I'll be fine." She wiped her hands on the back of her pants and tightened her ponytail.

Jade hoisted herself up easily. She didn't stop to wait for Kevin, but kept moving further and further up the cliff face. She was trying not to think about the consequences that if she slipped, the fall would kill her.

"You're getting too far ahead, wait up," Kevin called.

She was two ledges above him, off to his right and so close to the flow of the waterfall that she was getting wet from the spray. The water was still cold, and she shivered. Ignoring Kevin's pleas, like a machine she searched for the next handhold, the next foothold, getting closer and closer to the top of the waterfall and the caves where she hopes to find her father. Her mind was racing. Ignoring doubts and telling herself she could do it, Jade denied negative thoughts that tried to plague her. *You're clumsy; you're physically incompetent,* she heard. *You're not athletic. You're certainly no rock climber.* "Shut the hell up," she whispered to the voices in her mind, but they kept coming. *You're just a teenager, a human, nothing special. You won't defeat me. You will never find your father, never.* Jade dug her fingers into a hole in the rock and hung on. Whose voice was that? It wasn't hers. Jade lost focus, trying to shut out the voices. "Shut up!" she yelled.

"Jade," Kevin called. He scrambled up the rock face to get to her.

She hung on with three fingers of one hand and two fingers of the other. The toes of her shoes were wedged into the rock. The final cliff ledge she had to reach, hung just over her head and the two caves she had seen through the eyes of the eagle loomed above her, but they now seemed impossible to reach. She rested her brow on the cold wet stone, and cried; the darkness surrounding her was suddenly overbearing.

"Jade! I'm coming, hang on."

The strong grip of his hand around her ankle was reassuring. Why couldn't she have met him before the world turned to shit? Callie could have introduced them. He could have accompanied Callie to the United States, and while Callie worked in the laboratory as an undergraduate researcher for Jade's mom, Kevin could have attended school with Jade for the semester. He was smart enough. Things could have been so different. Everything was wrong, and nothing was good anymore; the world was empty of goodness. The thoughts barreled through her as she continued to sob for all of her loss. The urge to let go and crash to the rocks and snakes below was compelling. Who was she kidding; why did she think she could save her father? Intense dread and self-loathing grew from the pit of her stomach. She sensed something moving beside her, pushing past and hauling itself over the ledge above. Her mind drifted to a dark place of souls crying in pain, where the lost and the banished clamored in an ocean of tears, reaching out for someone to save them. One of them was her father, and she was never going to be able to go into that place and come back with him so she let go of the rock.

"What the hell are you doing, Jade?" Kevin yelled, panic evident in his voice. She was a dead weight, but Kevin was hanging onto her arm. It reminded her of Father McDonald and how he saved Casey from the fiery pit.

"Snap out of it," Kevin shouted down at her. "Put your feet back into the footholds. Jade wake up! Jade!"

She tilted her head up to Kevin to find him surrounded in light that was way too bright. The darkness of the place of lost souls had been so absolute that she had to look away from Kevin's light.

"Look at me, Jade. I can feel your emotions. You're being influenced by a dark force. You have to fight it. Come on, Jade. Fight it!" Kevin said, struggling to pull her up.

Her arms ached as he pulled and her chest scraped against the ragged edge, catching her t-shirt. She didn't care though. The darkness resurfaced. She belonged on the rocks below with the snakes and the lost souls. She was useless, worthless to society. Worthless.

But Kevin kept pulling her and wouldn't let go. He yanked her up and over the lip of the ledge to safety.

7

As quickly as they had descended upon her, the dark images floated away like a slow gray fog. Warmth began to fill her cheeks and she found Kevin's lips were pressed against hers. Her senses filled with images of abundance and flowers, blue skies, laughter, children, celebrations. She was filled with a giddy delight. Her blood turned to sparkling champagne. An overwhelming sensation of bubbly, addictive love filled her veins. Jade pressed back, returning his kiss and her body felt as if it was wrapped in an ethereal blanket that filled with illuminating colors and love.

Slowly, K pulled away, and Jade opened her eyes.

"You okay?" The tip of his tongue glided across his lip in remembrance. He bit down on his bottom lip, seeming to regret the kiss. "I'm sorry, I shouldn't have done that without permission. I didn't know what else to do to bring you back from the awful place that was blanketing you in despair," Kevin said. He winced, holding his arm.

"What is it?" She could barely speak. "My shoulder."

"It feels like it was dislocated," Jade managed to say.

She picked up his hand and holding his arm at the elbow said, "This is going to ..."

"Arghh ..." He screamed and danced on the spot, getting too close to the edge. He was cradling his arm. "Shit, that damn well killed," he panted.

"But, the shoulder feels better, right?" Jade said, looking concerned.

As the initial shock wore off, Kevin rubbed his arm and let out a sigh. "Sort of. Thanks."

"You're welcome. And thanks. I know where my dad is, and it's not going to be easy. That place of despair you saved me from? My dad's there somewhere. Did you feel what it was doing to me, K? That darkness just sucked everything good out and left nothing by hollow emptiness. It was crippling."

"Yes, It was frightening, I felt the emptiness inside you Jade."

"I have no idea how I'm going to get there and bring him back." Jade said.

"First, we have to find his body. We ought to keep moving," Kevin said, adjusting his backpack on his shoulders.

"You're right and..." Jade said, letting her words fade. Kevin waited. "And...?" he said, raising his eyebrows.

"Um, nothing. Come on, we'd better get moving. The sun's going down, and my mom is out there alone. I thought she would have caught up with us by now," Jade said, looking back over the forest.

"She's safe. I took her back to the Black Mountain campground, where we arrived through the portal."

THEY STOOD SIDE BY SIDE, CATCHING THEIR BREATH, ABSORBING the healing energy of the forest. "Did you know green is in the middle of the color spectrum and its frequency can have a calming effect on the mind and body? It creates a state of..." Jade's voice trailed off.

"I was just thinking of Casey. If he were here, he could have levitated us," Kevin said.

"Yeah, and we could have flown over the snakes," Jade said. "It's incredible what Casey can do. He made me feel like I had wings and I could fly. Do you think he can teach us how he does it when we get back to the estate?" Her logical mind told her that that would be impossible, but the hope of a future gave her strength. "We could use his help right about now, and Sophia's too."

"I don't think he could teach it. It's like what I do; it's just me. It's part of me and I can't transfer it, just like what Casey can do is unique to him. It's like you being smart and manipulating the weather, and time seems different around you since we returned the Emerald Tablet, and ..." He trailed off.

Tilting her head to one side she concentrated on his words. "I don't like the word manipulating," she said.

Then it all came back to her, the darkness, dark places, pain, scary nights, a place you would spend a lifetime avoiding, a place of nightmares. Jade, feeling freaked out, touched her lips to remember the warmth and energy of the kiss, of Kevin's kiss. It was crazy that a moment ago she was filled with joy and now she felt impending doom again. Something was out here trying to prevent them from getting too close, but she had to be stronger. Consciously, shifting her energy toward her solar plexus and away from her mind, she felt joy again. She wanted to mention the kiss and tell Kevin how good it made her feel. Whenever they were close or kissing, she felt all uncertainty melt away.

"Which cave?" she said.

"That cave," Kevin answered, confidently. He pointed to the cave furthest away.

"I agree, but that's a very narrow opening. I can't see how anyone could fit through there."

"I'm sure that's the cave." Kevin leaned his head forward as if searching harder.

A crawling sensation and goosebumps told her he was right.

She moved across the slippery rocks, avoiding the hanging icicles.

Kevin was close behind. The water traveled over rocks and under sheets of ice, and Jade thought to herself that if it wasn't so dangerous, it would have been beautiful. She was numb from the cold, but they continued until they were above the falls and standing on the icy shelf before the cave.

The feeling of a presence, lingering in front of the narrow opening, made Jade think of a negative version of Sophia's dome of protection, shielding Casey's estate from anyone passing.

"Do you think we are the future?" Jade asked, randomly, while moving toward the cave.

Kevin lifted his backpack from his sore shoulder and tossed it over his other shoulder. "I think you're stalling."

"I think our generation is the one that will start to use the dormant part of our brains. Well, what's left of our generation at least. I think knowledge of the body's healing potential will escalate, and we will be able to ignite new neural pathways in our brains to access qualities beyond the five senses..." She lingered at the front of the cave, where the barrier of energy started emanating dark magic through her. "Can you feel it?"

He didn't need to answer. He had taken two steps back. "Kevin?"

He took another step back, but she grabbed him before he toppled off the edge. "Careful," Jade said.

"The shield pushes outward and I was trying to feel where it ended. I'm sensing conflicting energies. One is an undercurrent of goodness and protection and the other..."

"What, K?"

His hair was soaked from the icy spray of the waterfall and he combed his fingers through it, thinking. He shivered as if someone or something had scared him. "The energy, it's like an evil spell or some- thing. I've never met a witch, a wizard, or a witch doctor, but this feels like something diseased," he said. He looked down to the body of water at the bottom of the waterfall. "This place gives me the creeps. It doesn't look so healing and inviting anymore."

For the first time, Jade suddenly understood what it was like for Kevin to feel someone else's deep emotions. Kevin's terrified feelings were jumping onto her like an electrical current and she could sense an evil presence lurking in a vast space, a place he didn't want to enter. He became aware of her spiritual presence connecting with his and brushed off her arm.

"I know that energy, but I haven't felt it for a very long time," he said. "A man who once lived in our street—we all called him the bogeyman—touched my arm, and I saw and felt the darkness inside of him. For a split second, I knew he had killed dozens of children, because I heard their screams and felt their pain. Their souls were trapped in a realm of despair, but the man, overnight, was gone. Jade, we shouldn't cross the threshold into the realm of despair. It's worse than death."

"I believe my dad is somewhere inside this cave. What if the energy shield is inciting your worst fear?" Jade asked.

"Well, it's doing a damn good job then," Kevin said. "I haven't thought about that man since I was nine years old."

"What if there is nothing to be frightened of? What if my dad is in there, and somebody created this shield with negative energy to imprison him. A shield to warn off people from entering the cave, to make us leave. I have to go inside, K... and I need you to come with me." Her eyes were pleading, waiting for him to answer. "The terrible feelings and visions I had, climbing up here, pushed me to my limits, and I let go of the cliff. If it wasn't for you, I would be lying at the bottom of the waterfall, broken. The desolation consumed me. I would have easily fallen to my death so if you don't come, who is going to save me?"

She stepped closer to the force field and could feel the misery. Tears pooled in her eyes as haunting sounds of her father screaming and her mother wailing filled her ears. Jade smelled burning flesh, so she pinched her nose and tried to shake the off the terrible feelings.

Behind the negative energy shield a bear moved as if underwater. Jade closed her eyes and searched the silence of her mind for the answer. She was going to have to squeeze into that narrow crack. She opened her eyes, and the hairs on her arms stood up. The deception of the shield kept trying to worm its way into her being, causing her to want to run and leap from the cliff to the frozen snakes below. She engaged her own voice of reason to step forward and analyze the situation, that it was just a facade, smoke and mirrors to prevent anyone from investigating further.

"We can't just stand here." She reached out her hand and physically touched the energy barrier. It was pulsating, definitely a shield. She pulled her hand back.

Wiggling her fingers, shaking her hands and bouncing on

her toes, Jade pumped up her confidence. Kevin put the backpack over both of his shoulders. She turned her head slightly toward him and peered out of the corner of her eye. Their hands and fingers intertwined and in one step they penetrated the translucent negative shield together, and entered the cave.

Jade's mouth dropped in awe. The hidden entrance was wide enough to drive a vehicle through. "I knew it!" Jade said, letting go of Kevin's hand and making a triumphant fist. "The small opening was just an illusion." Glancing over her shoulder, Jade looked back in wonderment. "But how?"

"I've stopped asking how, and instead I'm asking a lot more whys?" Kevin said. "Why is there a shield in front of the cave projecting a false impression of the entrance? Is the image of the small entry way to stop people from finding whatever's inside?"

"I think you're right," Jade said.

Kevin's torch blinked on and off. The light stabilized and shone into the mysterious cave that stretched out at least twenty feet in front of them. The sound of the waterfall outside was muffled. The air was humid and musty and the sound of their feet splashing as they stepped into puddles, bounced off the cave walls.

Fallen rocks lay in clusters toward the back of the cave. The darkness swimming in her vision made it hard to see beyond the shadows. Her heart was feeling uplifted and the sense of despair had vanished. The shield was smart. *Had the grim shaman set up another trap*, she wondered? It would be good to one day find a respectable healer to teach her, instead of having one who attacked her. How awesome would that be? She laughed, thinking maybe Merlin would appear to her. *Yeah, right*, she thought, *just like a troll is going to step out from behind the rocks seeking payment*. She was losing focus as they walked deeper into the cave.

As her eyes adjusted a little more to the dark, she silenced the nonsense inside her head as she came across a group of bears sleeping. Jade edged forward for a closer look and found that instead of bears, they were nothing more than a cluster of rocks sparkling in the light. *She had to stop seeing bears everywhere*, she thought. Jagged amethyst stones were reflected in Kevin's flashlight beam as he swept the light across the ceiling and floor of the cave.

"A dead end. A boulder has sealed the entrance to this passage," he said approaching a large rock.

Nervously, Jade stepped forward, her feet splashing in the puddles. The light from outside, or the sound of the waterfall, couldn't be seen or heard this far into the cave. She listened to the air squishing out of the soles of her shoes as she moved. Her shoes and socks were soaked, making her wish she was in front of a warm fire at Casey's, and she imagined herself laughing with Sophia and Casey. She had never had any real friends before. School had been so hard. Being smart and an introvert wasn't the best combination for getting invited to parties. She also imagined her mom and dad safe in Casey's kitchen, talking with Joe and Terry; the soul kitchen. That's never going to happen unless she finds her dad. He called out to her, and not her mother... there had to be a reason why. He could already be dead—perhaps this was a trap to kill her too. Think positively, be tenacious, adventurous, and have certainty. What was it Sophia had said while searching for the Emerald Tablet? Certainty beyond reason, be positive, and have optimistic thoughts? Bring them on, Jade thought.

Akin to the petals of a flower unfolding, the energy centers in her body tingled, and she remembered the feeling of K's soft, gentle lips pressed against hers. She touched her bottom lip with her index finger and breathed deeply, drawing on the beautiful feeling the memory gave her.

"Jade, what are you thinking about?" Kevin said with a look of curiosity.

She had forgotten for a second how hypersensitive he was to people's emotions and felt embarrassed. Jade cleared her throat, and said, "I am trying to stay calm. I'm worried it might be a trap, and that we're doomed."

He looked at her as if he knew what she'd really been feeling and thinking. "I think there's more of that bad magic in the cave and it's meant to confuse us; to make us lose focus and maybe get lost. If that's the case, there has to be a way past the blockage. I won't let anything happen to you, Jade, I won't let anyone or anything hurt you. You're not going to die, Jade, but..." He turned away from searching for a passageway and hugged her.

"But what, K?" Jade asked, suddenly agitated and stepping out from his embrace.

"... a piece of you will die," he said.

"What do you mean? Like frostbite? Leprosy?" said Jade. "Well, don't leave me hanging."

Without warning, from the direction of the dead end, a colony of bats rushed from behind the boulder, flapping, clicking, and scratching.

"Kevin!" Jade squatted down and covered her head. The bats swarmed around them. Jade screamed in pain as one dug its thumb-like hooks into her back. The bats flapped their wings, the outstretched skin slapping her on arms and torso. We've disturbed a roost, she thought, as she felt the bats' hairy legs and bony arms. It was hideous. It was like the bats had been set upon them. Kevin smacked them away with his torch and cocooned her with his body. He was receiving the full force of the bats' rage. His head yanked away from hers as a bat pulled at his hair. A substantial portion of the colony exited the cave, but, for a while, two kept clawing and biting Kevin on the arms and back.

Finally, stillness returned, but they stayed huddled together on the ground. Kevin waved his arms above his head one more time checking the bats were gone. At some point, he had dropped his torch and it had rolled toward the back of the cave from where the bats had emerged. Dazed, he scrambled across the cave floor and banged his knee on some stones sticking up from the ground.

"Hey, there's an opening here, Jade," he said out of breath. "It's not a dead end."

He was unsteady, slightly wavering, as he went to help her. Blood dripped from her arms and her hair was a mess. "I have to sit down," she said, leaning back against the wall. It was reassuring; nothing could attack her from behind. She could feel the veins in her neck, pulsating.

"Arghhh! For god's sake!" Jade screamed. "Every step of the way we're being prevented from moving forward. This is bullshit!" Blood dripped onto her face. Absentmindedly, she wiped it off. Then, worried it would splash into her eyes, she looked up and squinted to see where it was coming from. Kevin was standing over her, his arm outstretched to brace himself against the wall. He was unstable and appeared as if he was going to faint. Blood was dripping from his head and arms. "K, sit down. You're bleeding." Jade pulled him down to sit beside her.

He raised his hand. Touching his head, feeling for the source of the blood, he found that a patch of his hair was missing. He pulled his hand away, only to see it was covered in blood. "Shit! Bloody vampire bats. The son of a bitch took a chunk out of me." Jade quickly searched his head for injuries, finding two deep gashes. "You're going to need a rabies shot and stitches. You're lucky you didn't get scalped. We need to get you back to mom now," Jade said with urgency. His jacket was torn along the arms. "Give me your jacket." Jade cut a strip from the lower back and tied it like a bandanna around his head to help with the bleeding. "Don't you die on me, Kevin." Her words came out forcefully, masking her panic.

She then cut the arms off the jacket to create four bandages. She cleaned up her own arm as best she could and used the rest for the wounds on Kevin's arms. He smiled as she attended to his cuts, but he agreed that he was definitely going to need a rabies shot. He was already grinning deliriously by the time he put the armless jacket back on and zipped it up.

"I'm not going anywhere without you. I'll survive. Let's just get going and find your dad."

Jade was torn. He needed medical attention, but if they left, she was sure she would never see her dad again. "Half an hour, and then we go back. What do you think?"

"We find your dad, and then we go back," Kevin said, walking off toward the boulder.

They both squeezed through the crack where the bats had come from. The cave continued to stretch before them and sloped down, leading deeper underground.

"Kevin, wait a minute. Before the bats, what were you going to say? You said a part of me was going to die."

He massaged his shoulder, before adjusting the strap on the backpack. His shirt rode up at the back and Jade saw diagonal claw marks across his spine, just above his cargo pants. His whole back could have been badly scratched if he hadn't been wearing the pack during the attack.

"K, your back!"

"It's nothing," he said, tugging his shirt down.

She searched his face and saw that he was in pain and afraid. He looked at his hands and bent down to clean the blood off them in a puddle. He dried them on the bottom of his pants. He was avoiding eye contact, letting his fringe flop over his eye. He watched her with one eye and said, "I see it like this, snakes shed skin, but they don't die. Sometimes it's hard to articulate what I feel. It's like you have to shed a layer of skin or something," he said, touching his stomach as if he felt sick.

Shaking her head as if to clear it, Jade said, "You know what, it doesn't matter what happens to me. We need to get you help. We have to go back."

"No. We're not going back," Kevin said.

"At least give me the bag." Jade reached up to Kevin's shoulder to take the backpack, and he winced again in pain. "I only have my notebook, a torch and a drink in my pack. I'll put my stuff in yours, roll my bag up and squash it in as well."

He didn't argue. "This way," said Kevin.

Jade followed Kevin deeper into the cave, toward the faint light. Sparkling gemstones bulged from the walls as Kevin scanned from left to right before lingering on the ceiling. He was checking for vampire bats, Jade was sure of it. If they got out of this alive, he was going to have problems with bats, perhaps anything that flew and swooped like birds, or even insects, for a while. A bug startled her from her reverie and she slapped at her face.

Jade started to pick up her pace to walk beside Kevin. "How are you feeling?"

He mumbled a reply.

He's been bitten by vampire bats. How do you think he feels? Jade didn't want to stop worrying about Kevin, but she had to. She needed to focus on the power of the bear, hush the internal chatter and tune in to the energy waves—those feelings inside her body that could flow from her etheric energy centers; chakras—so she would know the answers from the Great Void. She had to find her father, and get help for Kevin. She didn't know what she would do if she had to choose between the two of them. Kevin was now a significant part of her life and that was not something she thought would happen to her.

THEY HAD COME TO THE END. THERE WAS NOWHERE ELSE TO go. Jade relaxed her mind and absorbed the stillness of the cave. Relaxing her breathing, she drew an imaginary golden line running from her feet to the top of her head and pulled it upward, as Sophia had taught her. The muscles in her back and shoulders relaxed and her breathing sounded like she was asleep. In the distance, she heard the slow rhythmic beat of a drum pounding behind her heart. She moved toward the cave wall and placed her hand on the cool, flickering stones. Her body moved in concert with her hands as she slid her palms slowly down the wall, until her hands lost contact with it and met the thin air of a hole. Losing her balance, she lunged forward, smacking the side of her face against the cold stone. Kevin shone the torch to find her hands had disappeared into a large opening which looked like a fox's den. The memory of the fox wrapped around the shaman's neck alarmed her. She quickly pulled her hands out and held them to her chest. *This could be a trap after all*, she thought.

The aroma of incense was drifting through the fox's den from a slight breeze inside the cave. She took hold of Kevin's torch. The tunnel was winding; it turned slightly to the left then back to the right like a dry, winding riverbed.

Someone was burning sage; she could smell it. No one could sit upright in the den for long, there had to be an exit into another part of the cave. Jade swung the backpack around and put it on her chest. They were going to have to crawl. "I'll keep the torch," Jade said, shoving it into her bra strap, and making adjustments so it would shine forward, like a torch attached to a combat vest.

"That's cool. You're clever, I never would have done that," Kevin said.

"Of course, you would have."

"No, because I don't wear a bra." He Jested.

She smiled at him. "Stay close," she instructed.

The muscle under his eye twitched. Suddenly irritated, he scratched at his arm, around the wounds. He lifted up the makeshift bandaging and spat on his wounds. "Saliva can help; it has antibacterial properties," he said. He pulled what was left of his windbreaker over his head, obviously feeling warm.

Jade rolled up the jacket, shoving it into the front pocket of the pack and noticed a first-aid kit. "Why didn't you tell me you had a basic medical kit?"

"You –"

"Whatever the answer is, it's not going to change anything now. Stay close," she said and crawled into the narrow opening. The air was stale, and smelled like wet dog. There were tiny bones, probably rats, making her reluctant to move forward. She shuffled a few feet and turned back to make sure Kevin was able to fit. His shoulders were broader, but he cleared the entrance by about two inches. It was tight and suffocating.

Jade crawled deeper into the tunnel for only a minute or two before she needed to stop to calm herself down. Her heart was racing and she was panting, using up way to much oxygen. If she didn't calm down she was going to hyperventilate. She cleaned her hands on her cargos before she continued. The tunnel was long, it felt like they were moving downward and she was afraid they would run out of air.

"It's really stuffy and hot in here," Kevin said.

She looked over her shoulder. He was struggling, his hair soaked from sweat. She paused to pull her ponytail tight and forced herself to maintain a slow pace. She wanted to rush away from the oppressive walls. *In through the nose and out through the mouth*, she chanted inside her head to settle her breathing. Maybe this was another bad idea. They had been crawling through the tunnel for over ten minutes and her hands were starting to bleed due to the rough, rocky ground. There was nowhere to turn around, so going back wasn't an option.

A cough pounded in her chest. She tried to stifle the urge, but had to stop and cough until she nearly passed out. Kevin was heavily perspiring and his breathing was rapid. The sound of a drum entered the tunnel from up ahead, and the smell of herbs was getting stronger.

"Turn off the torch," Kevin said. "What! Why?"

"I sense there's someone beyond the next curve." He rubbed his face against his shoulder to wipe the sweat away. He coughed and his body curled over.

Jade could see he was trying to get it together. He nodded as if ready. She fumbled with the torch, held firm in the twisted bra strap, to turn out the light. The cave was as black as ink at first, but a faint glow of light reached out to them from beyond the next curve.

The backpack hung from her stomach like a pot belly and was scraping along the ground. She stopped to tighten the straps to keep it up. She stuck close to the edge of the curve to spy on whomever or whatever was around the bend since it could be the shaman and his men waiting for her, to take her power—power she hadn't even known she had. Great Turtle and her mother knew, and maybe her dad knew; that's why he called out to her. There wasn't any weather inside a cave to control—no clouds, wind, rain or trees—so how could that ability help to protect Kevin and herself? How could she make the rain fall, or the snow fall, or make sunshine so bright it's blinding, from inside a cave a mile underground? She could feel a slight breeze drifting into the tunnel from around the bend. She bottled her dread, drew strength from her frustration, and brazenly peered around the curve.

A FEW FEET IN FRONT OF HER WAS THE EXIT FROM THE FOX'S den where a small fire radiated a soft light. She felt like she was spying through a window into someone's home. Drumming by the fire was Chief Thundercloud. He looked the same, but he always appeared the same. From the first day she had seen him out front of her house after her mother was kidnapped two years ago, to yesterday, when she saw him outside her house on their arrival through the portal from the estate. He looked exactly like he did under the tree. His clothes had changed, the environment had changed, but he never seemed to age. He always looked like an old man; Jade imagined he was probably in his seventies.

She knew she had changed and she certainly felt a lot older than sixteen. It had been over nine months since she attended school. It was sad, because she liked learning; she was a sponge in the classroom and learning came easily to her, but school would never be the same again. Her eyes fixed on a boot partly hidden by the bulk of Chief Thunder-cloud. A man, obscured from view, was lying on the ground beside him. *It must be her dad!* In her excitement she had to stop herself from rushing out of the tunnel and into the new chamber of the cave. Chief Thundercloud has her dad! He wouldn't harm him, would he? She had told her dad on the phone in Callie's house, the day Kevin had found her, to go with the American Indian and that he would keep him safe. *It's all my fault*, she thought in horror. If she hadn't told him to go with Chief Thundercloud, maybe he would have been safe at home when they had arrived through the portal.

Pressing against the tunnel wall, she shuffled backwards, feeling her way to Kevin. Straining her neck to see over her shoulder and beyond the dark, she turned on the torch, worried she might hit him in the face. She shone the light to find him face down in the dirt.

"Kevin, wake up." Jade turned on her side and wriggled in next to him. Softly, she touched his shoulder with a trembling hand. He was on fire, the heat radiated off of him in waves. She parted his fringe and checked his wounds under the bandage to find the blood was congealing. He had two deep gashes: they looked dark and moist like sap. He urgently needed stitches, antibiotics, a rabies shot. He was already running a fever. It was going to be near impossible to get him out of the cave. She couldn't push him, and she couldn't pull him backward. "Kevin ... Kevin, you have to get up."

Kevin mumbled "No. Let me sleep, Mom. You're such a

nag, let me sleep." The dirt was damp from the drool leaking out of his mouth.

"What?" Jade said, hoping she had just misunderstood him. "Kevin, what's wrong? Talk to me."

"Alex, buddy!"

Jade lowered her voice and spoke as quietly as possible. "K, it's me, Jade. Open your eyes, K." Kevin was weak and hallucinating.

"Come on, wake up. It's just a few feet and you'll be out of the tunnel."

Her head was throbbing from the heat their bodies generated in the small space. "I'm sorry, Kevin, but I have to do this." She slapped him in the face, hoping to shock him into action. She needed to get him out of the tunnel. She didn't want to imagine how much pain he must be in. She slapped him again, harder.

His eyes flew open; they were red and angry. "What the hell did you do that for?"

"Move it, Kevin. Move, now!"

His eyes rolled in his head and he passed out. She thought of mentioning Alex, to make him angry and move, but she couldn't be so cruel; he missed his little brother. There wasn't much she could do.

She had to leave him there.

8

Jade watched Chief Thundercloud. She was reluctant to leave the safety of the tunnel, even though it was giving her terrible feelings of claustrophobia. She was also afraid her dad was dead. The pain would be too much. She didn't want Kevin to die either. Jade reversed back and squeezed in next to him again. She lay with her hand on his back and cried. Softly, she kissed the cheek she had slapped. "I'll be back for you. I promise." He mumbled something as if he knew she was there.

As she exited the tunnel, the man turned toward her.

"Are you Chief Thundercloud?" she asked. "You told me to come. You promised I would find my father. Is that my father beside you?" She looked around the cave, which was much larger than she guessed initially. It looked like it had been his home for some time, because there were metal pots and pans, gas burners, blankets, washing bowls and four ten-gallon water coolers with taps, along with bundles of water bottles, shrink-wrapped and stacked close to the ceiling. Crates were used to support planks of wood that were set up as a tabletop. There were a couple of tunnels running off the main chamber. A faint breeze was still coming from somewhere. The air was better than inside the fox tunnel and she drew in a deep, jagged breath, but stayed by the entrance of the den, primed to flee. He stopped drumming. "I've been waiting for you, Raven Wings. To find your father, you must travel to the Realm of Lost Souls."

"But my dad's right next to you. I need look no further," she said, taking a step forward.

"Your friend is sick."

"Yes. He's passed out. I'm afraid he'll die," Jade said.

"He was bitten by vampire bats," Chief Thundercloud stated. "Yes."

How did he know about Kevin? How long has he been aware of us? He probably heard her coughing. It was only twenty feet or less to where Kevin had passed out in the tunnel.

"Can you help him, please? I will give you my power for the life of my father and Kevin." Her voice quavered, hoping her power was something of true value.

He put down his drum. "I don't want the burden of your power." He picked up a bunch of herbs, plucked a few buds. He popped them into his mouth before uncrossing his legs and standing. He reached for a bundle of rope, threaded his arm through the middle of the coil and hoisted it onto his shoulder. Jade had never noticed how tall he was before. His hands went to his waist and he started to undo the buckle on his belt. He walked silently toward her as he drew the belt tight and refastened it. The belt was covered in turquoise stones and beads. It was beautiful—red, blue, and white and probably handcrafted. It reminded her of the shaman's head band. She had no time to get back into the tunnel as he approached, so she readied herself with her hand hovered at her side ready to draw her bowie knife. He stopped a foot away and created a lasso with the rope.

"Put this around your friend's shoulders, pull one arm through, and make sure it is secure so it doesn't ride up and choke him or break his neck. I will pull him out."

Jade relaxed her hand. She studied the man and decided he was her only hope. She had to trust him so she dropped the backpack and slowly reached for the rope.

She hustled back into the claustrophobic tunnel.

The smell of Kevin's sickly feverish perspiration was at least masking the smell of wet dog. He lay unconscious and she struggled with the rope, forcing it over his head. He was a dead weight and she was drained of energy. Finally, she managed to pull his arm through the loop. As soon as she had him in the right position, she began to move back down the tunnel, at the same time she yelled, "Pull! Pull slowly now!" As the rope went taut beneath her, Chief Thunder-cloud's strength surprised her. The rope burned her stomach as it jerked and yanked Kevin toward her. She hadn't noticed it had caught underneath her.

"Stop!" She paused, and waited for the rope to go slack. As she moved back toward the bend, before the exit, she could hear the cracks in the rock whistling. On her knees she faced Kevin and braced herself. "Okay. Pull," she yelled, and coughed. The dust in the cave floated in the light beams above Kevin's head. The darkness behind him scared her. Anything could be coming toward him. For some reason, she imagined a vicious dog biting down on his leg and pulling him into the darkness. She had to shake the images out of her mind. Kevin's face and stomach grazed against tiny shards of rock with each tug.

He was going to be so battered and bruised by the time they made it home. His mom and dad, everyone, would fuss over him. *This time tomorrow we'll be home*, she thought, *eating a slice of Joe's moist, boiled fruitcake with custard*. When Chief Thundercloud halted, she dropped her head on the ground and gave herself a second before moving around the corner to the mouth of the cave.

She wiped her face and yelled over her shoulder. "Pull!" What if he's had a heart attack? She should be out there helping him, she thought to herself before the rope tensed and he pulled with even greater strength. Kevin's head was at the corner, his side scraping against the curve. It was only a few more feet to go so Jade crawled out, as Chief Thundercloud waited for her to stand clear of the exit.

"One more pull," she said.

Kevin's head stuck out of the hole, lifeless and bloody. He looked so bad. She crouched down and tried to find a pulse.

"Kevin! You can't die. K, wake up!" She could hear in her voice that what little strength she had left was fading.

Chief Thundercloud pulled her to her feet to move her out of the way. He reached under Kevin's armpits and pulled him out, then he lifted him up and laid him by the crackling fire. Chief Thundercloud placed his large weatherworn hands on both sides of Kevin's skull as if blocking out all sound. He lifted the young man's head slightly to spit herbs on his crown and then examined Kevin's wounds. The Chief laid Kevin's head down gently and drew back his eyelids to check the whites of his eyes, which were reddish-yellow. He proceeded to roll Kevin partly on his side to inspect the gruesome scratches carved into his back.

"I need to clean and treat his wounds," he said.

Jade turned to her dad and reached out to touch his arm.

"Don't touch! You must wait. Your aura must be cleansed; you have been drugged. I see in your aura that you have a hole that must be closed; then you will need to prepare to save your father's soul. First, we'll give your friend a chance to live," he said, picking up a canvas satchel.

Jade drew her hand from her father and wiped away her tears. She focused on Chief Thundercloud cleaning out Kevin's wounds as he lay unconscious. "Will he be okay?"

"I promise nothing. I will try. He has great spirit medicine within him."

Jade watched Chief Thundercloud remove different herbs from his bag and lay them out. "Can I help?"

"Get the jug of water and cloth," he pointed to his

supplies and continued with his instruction, "to clean his arms. Then boil some more water. Use the water in the container next to the pile of wood."

She did as he asked and stayed quiet while he mixed up the herbs and chanted. Jade recognized a few plants; she saw sage, heart-of-the-earth or self-heal, willow bark, lavender, rhubarb root, Echinacea—which Great Turtle had grown and called purple coneflower. He must have had at least ten different types of plants laid out in front of him. There were tiny bottles of oils and jars with powders and teas as well. Observing her surroundings, it seemed as if he had been here in his healing cave for some time. She looked at the shelves cut into the stone and saw a wooden box decorated as a child might, with shells and stones. It looked out of place among the assortment of jars and remedies. Recent kills of rabbit and raccoon hung from a meat hook. There must be another entrance to the cave for Chief Thundercloud to go hunting and to have brought all this stuff in here. A blanket lay against the wall close to her father and she assumed it was where Thundercloud slept.

She watched as he busied himself, caring for Kevin. "Can you get me the bottle of purple coneflower on the second shelf over there?" He pointed to the jars and bottles she had been scanning.

"Sure." She got up and went to the shelf cut in the wall. Some of the bottles and jars looked very old. She read the labels, seeing snake venom, peyote, nutmeg and marshmallow, cedar and sandalwood.

"Stop gawking. You will have plenty of time later," Chief Thundercloud said.

Jade found the bottle of Echinacea, and Chief Thundercloud poured some over Kevin's wounds.

Jade studied her father from the other side of the crackling fire. She was afraid to get closer. He was still breathing... she could see the slight rise and fall of his chest. *He's alive.* She glanced up at the chief and said, "What happened to him?"

"Pick up that bowl and mix juniper berries, sage leaves and lavender flower. Boil them together in a small pot to make a healing brew for your aura, body, mind and spirit. You must drink it all."

Jade looked at him unsure. The last potion she drank was probably what caused the hole in her aura.

"Why do you hesitate, Raven Wings?" he said, picking fresh self- heal leaves and applying them to the wounds on Kevin's head.

"There is a shaman searching for me to steal my power. He lured me to an underwater cave and drugged me," she said. "It was my fault. I should have left as soon as I saw them."

"You were probably given the secretions from the gland of a toad, or a fungi potion. It would have kept you still long enough to extract your spiritual essence." He stopped what he was doing and studied the area around her. "Great Turtle entrusted me with gifts for you. But first you must drink while I finish with your friend. One day you will be a great medicine woman, like Great Turtle."

Jade collected the herbs and boiled the water. Sipping the potion slowly, she felt a little spooked, but her mind cleared and she felt like she was gaining strength. The dizziness and headache she had felt coming on in the tunnel was easing. She felt calm and was thankful it was nothing like the palpitations, or the heaviness and sense of panic she experienced from the shaman's potion.

"Now you must play the drum. Pick up that drum leaning against the wall, Raven Wings."

Jade touched it. It looked familiar.

"It was made by Great Turtle for you." Chief Thundercloud scooped ants into a jar. "Go into the spiral. You must do the dance of the sharp-tailed grouse. Your father is missing part of his soul and you have to find it before the soul-sucking demon finds it. You need to bring it back and blow it into your father's body through a vortex of etheric energy at his chest, which healers call the heart chakra."

Jade looked at him, dumbfounded. She had no idea how to do the dance of the grouse or find a missing part of her dad's soul. "What's a soul-sucking demon?"

"You will find out soon enough. Finish your brew. I need to focus on channeling healing energy for your friend."

She put the drum down where she had been sitting and picked up her nearly empty bowl. Bits of sage stuck between her teeth as she finished it off.

The movement of the pestle grinding the herbs against the mortar was hypnotizing. Chief Thundercloud added more herbs to his mix and pounded on the plants to make a paste. He removed the self-healing leaves and applied the paste to Kevin's head, arms, and back. He separated the boiled water into two bowls, and into one of them he added the leaves and roots.

Jade recognized willow bark as he added it with other plants to the second bowl. He dipped a piece of cloth into the first bowl and gently cleaned the scratches on Kevin's face. Then he rolled up another batch of self-healing leaves and soaked them in the liquid, before applying them to Kevin's face and brow. She imagined they were to reduce his fever, even though he had used warm water. *At least the water was sterile*, she thought.

"You have much to learn, Raven Wings. I was told you were clever, but you remember nothing of your family tradition. Pick up the drum now. You need to build up the energy in here. I will tell you of the old ways and what you must do."

She studied the drum. It felt uncomfortable in her hands, so she rested it on her crossed legs. She picked up the drumstick, which was a crooked pale-gray branch, half the size of her forearm. It was smooth to the touch and had fluffy sheepskin wrapped around its head. Gently, she placed the drumstick beside her. With a delicate touch, she laid her hand on the center of the drum's taut deerskin top. Connecting. Feeling something she didn't understand, but it came to her. Her other hand gripped the waxed string crisscrossing like a web on the underside, which held the skin taut around the circular wooden frame.

The memory of her and her great-grandmother making drums filled her mind. She pictured Great Turtle's strong face as she washed the skins, punched the holes with her knife, and stretched the skin over a circular cedar frame, before weaving the waxed string and pulling it tight—all while singing, laughing and telling stories about the deer and Great Spirit. Afterward, as the drums were drying, Jade painted a yellow symbol of the drum with wings on to a stone, and polished it.

Jade noticed something was tucked inside the back of the drum; it was a black feather—a raven's wing. It was attached to a long braid of all the colors of the rainbow, although underneath, it was hair. Her hair. She recalled her great-grandmother cutting the strands from her head before Jade started school. It was summer, and she'd stayed with Great Turtle at her log cabin in the mountains, while her parents worked. The first night of the three month stay, Great Turtle had braided a few strands of Jade's hair with fine, colored threads. Jade got to select each color, but Great Turtle then placed each color in a designated order because each color had its own empowering attributes and stories. This was the same piece of hair Great Turtle had cut from her head that first night. And that's the last time she had seen it 'till now. The gold was as bright as it was that day; the red, blue, green, and violet, were all just as vibrant. Jade ran her fingers over the hair. She had forgotten about the braid and now, here it is on the drum Chief Thundercloud had handed her, the drum Great Turtle made for her.

She pulled the braid and the feather out from behind the weave and let it dangle between her crossed legs. The drumstick was by her side, and she reached for it. Jade ran the woolen head of the stick in a clockwise circle on the drum. Lightly, she tapped the center. The wool gave it a soft, low muffled tone, but she was wary of the power of the drum if she hit it harder.

Chief Thundercloud stood and picked up his seashell, the one she remembered him using to burn herbs. He must have it always lit and smoking. He signaled for her to stand and with an expanding white wing splayed like a fan, he smudged her by moving the wing back and forth, circling her body and chanting. She was sad she didn't understand his words, but she lowered her head respectfully. A nervous sensation filled her solar plexus causing a need to pee. He blew the smoke in her face and told her to breathe in deeply, but she was anxious and feared she was going to have an asthma attack so she held her breath.

"You cannot hold your breath forever," Chief Thundercloud said. "Release yourself, Raven Wings. Death is not what you should fear."

Jade knew he was right—she couldn't hold her breath forever, so she puckered her lips and drew in the smallest breath. She was paranoid as she then breathed in through her nose and let the smoke trail deep into her lungs. Her chest expanded, but there was no cough. Jade signed in relief as she blew out.

She sat back down and picked up the drum, but she was hesitant, for fear of its power. She tapped on the drum, testing it and noticed that different parts of the drum produced different tones. Building confidence, she found a spot that she liked the sound of. She let her wrist relax into the rhythm and her drumming quickened. The feeling of the vibration filled the cave and her being. Her spirit was awakening. She accentuated certain beats, changing the rhythm. It was as if she had done this before and that feeling inspired her to go faster and faster. The resonance fascinated her and she lifted the drum to her ear, listening to the sound, expecting the reverberation to mess with her inner balance, but it didn't. She held back a childish giggle, feeling drunk on the energy the drum produced. She felt invincible and started to close her eyes, wanting to float upon the sound waves into infinity.

"Not yet Raven Wings, not yet," Chief Thundercloud said. "Slow down your beats, open your eyes slowly and ground yourself. Don't startle your spirit. Slow down the drumming and become aware of your body. Connect to Mother Earth and anchor yourself."

He tapped her on the elbow twice, just like Great Turtle and her mother had done whenever she was engrossed in a book; they had worried they would startle her. Once or twice it was like being flicked with an elastic band over her whole body.

The jar of ants was now empty. Jade wondered where they'd gone as she watched Chief Thundercloud go toward the shelf. He reached down behind a crate and brought out a small leather bag. He sat facing her with the leather bag between them and Jade studied it as if it was a specimen. As she gazed upon it, she noticed that it had leather drawstrings with white, yellow and black beads. The bag was about fifteen inches deep and six inches wide, like a long, wide sock.

"This is your sacred medicine pouch," he said.

"I've never seen that before," she said. Her brow wrinkled in wonderment. She looked over to Kevin. His breathing was calm, but his face and arms were red and raw; they looked to be inflamed. He was covered in beads of sweat. Looking over toward her dad, she spotted a twitch fall upon his face, as if having a nightmare.

"Okay, what do I have to do, how do I find him?" Jade said.

"Don't be the bull at the gate. Slow down," he said, tapping her on the elbow again.

Her attention turned back to him instantly. What was he doing? It seemed there was a focus point on her elbow; Jade thought her mother, and Great Turtle, had some explaining to do.

"We have to get them both to hospital," she said.

"Focus on the pouch," he said tilting his head down toward it. "Pick it up," he said calmly.

"It doesn't belong to me. I've never seen it before," she said.

"Don't be afraid. This is your medicine. Do not show the contents to anyone, it may lessen the power; it is your secret medicine power. One day you will learn how to use all your gifts—if you return from the Realm of Lost Souls. Not many medicine men have the power to travel to the other realms. That's why the shaman is hunting you; for your power." His eyes were serious. "Traveling to the Realm of Lost Souls could kill you, or leave you in a coma, like your father."

JADE PICKED UP THE SMALL POUCH AND FELT THE SOFTNESS OF the brown, yellow, and black scaly leather. It was no wider than her two hands side by side and had a diamond pattern. *What magic could be inside?* But then she remembered Shaun's pouch, and the gemstones it carried. Those gemstones were the key to closing the gate to the underworld, giving the human race a second chance. To underestimate the contents of the pouch might be a mistake, so Jade slowly pulled apart the leather drawstrings and poured some of the contents into her hand.

A piece of silk cloth tied up with waxed string fell out first. Jade untied the bow exposing its content. A snake's head and a collection of tiny vertebrae were sitting in the palm of her hand. Instinctively, she wanted to drop them and wipe her hand on her clothes, but as soon as she pushed them with her index finger, another memory came flooding back. How much of her life had she actually forgotten? Were they forgotten? Had she repressed the memories, or had they been hidden from her? So many questions?

"They are snake vertebrae," said Chief Thundercloud.

Jade knew he was right. She saw herself as a two-year-old reaching for a rattlesnake's rattle. As a two-year-old she had no sense of fear, no urge to run away. Surely she had known it was a snake, but as she watched the memory unfold, she felt the pain of the snake's fangs penetrating her arm. As a two-year-old, Jade was always curious.

Great Turtle had moved faster than the snake, capturing it, choking it, as it wrapped its body around her forearm. Her grandmother had carried her in one arm, and the snake in the other, back inside her log cabin. The poison had run through Jade's veins and quickly went to her heart. Great Turtle administered her sacred medicine and within days, Jade was walking around the property looking under bushes for more snakes as if nothing happened all while that snake hung from the rafters of the porch.

Jade was holding a black stone with a drawing of a snake eating its own tail, while Jade's great-grandmother dismembered the snake in front of her. As she had separated the different parts of the snake, she explained how to use them for medicine. They had crushed up the ribs, made a pouch— which she now held—and they had made a potion from the venom. Jade watched her two-year-old self and thought how strange it would have looked to an outsider, and she wondered if her parents had known.

Jade peered into the blue, twenty-five milliliter glass bottle in her hand that she had filled fourteen years ago. It contained what looked like sand-flakes; it must be the crushed ribs. There was a smaller brown glass bottle, also about fifteen milliliters, and she knew it contained the potion. Jade quickly put the bottles back in the pouch. Looking inside, she discovered the snakeskin pouch also accommodated leather wrist straps, the snake's rattle, gemstones, crystal dust, and the onyx stone with the drawing of the snake eating its own tail. She pulled out and studied the stone, turning it over in her hand. It was smooth and a burning sensation filled her arm as the flash of a snake appeared in front of her, reared up as if to strike. Jade recoiled and immediately put down the stone. The vision of the snake vaporized as quickly as it had appeared. Prepared for any forgotten memories to arise, she cautiously touched the rim of the singing bowl with a wooden mallet. The copper singing bowl fitted nicely in the palm of her hand and Jade tapped the bowl; she then remembered tapping, or flicking, it whenever she had visited her great-grandmother in the mountains. The singing bowl had a majestic, resonant tone, which always resembled monks chanting high in the Tibetan mountains when she heard it. Jade took all the items from the pouch again, placed them inside the bowl and gently slid the bowl into the pouch, sticking the wooden mallet down the side.

"You now have most of the tools to ignite your mystical powers," Chief Thundercloud said, while reaching into his duffel bag. "You may or may not need these tools today, but they are part of your medicine. You have the gentleness of the deer, and the power of introspection from the bear, access to the womb-cave and the void, the raven's magic, the snake's transmutation, and the power of creation. Also, the medicine of the turtle, the spirit of Mother Earth, and the sight of the eagle; but today, you will need to learn the dance of the sharp-tailed grouse. You may also need a guiding light."

In his hands he held out a rod, or a wand of sorts. It was covered in green suede with vines of willow snaking from top to bottom. At each end of the rod was a clear quartz crystal. The end she assumed to be the top, had fluffy white feathers attached. Down the spine, nestled in spirals of willow vine, were gemstones. The base had a piece of fur wrapped around it that she guessed would be from a bear.

"That crystal allows you to take many journeys into multiple dimensions. It is a Terminator Crystal with windows into different realms. The feathers are male grouse feathers," Chief Thundercloud said. "The wand will help you awaken and center your personal power. There are nine gemstones; those include amethyst, blue agate, raw emerald, turquoise, rose quartz, citrine, jasper, smoky quartz, and black onyx."

It was mesmerizing. Holding the wand, she felt the power, like a subtle current of electrical energy. She held it to her chest, hugging it tightly. She was enshrouded with fellowship; it was like she had found something precious she had lost long ago.

"There is no time to explain all the properties of your wand," the Chief said.

She looked at her dad and his body trembled. "Why can't you help him? If you know all that I need to know, why haven't you saved him?" She felt disrespectful, but she had to ask. "Why all the charades and rituals?"

"I don't have your power. As I said, not every medicine man has your gift to travel to the different realms without taking peyote—and some would kill for it. We are not of the same blood, Raven Wings. Your bloodline possesses the power to enter the sacred spiral into the Realm of Lost Souls. Only you can find your father and destroy the beast that seeks the lost part of his soul," the chief said.

"Then why not my mother? Why was she not called to this place?"

"It is a special magic which skips generations and you are the last one to carry the secrets in your blood," the chief said. "Come, Raven Wings, you are wasting time."

9

K evin's body started to convulse. He was foaming at the mouth and bile trailed down his chin. "Quickly, Thundercloud, help him." Jade laid down the wand and scrambled over to Kevin. Chief Thundercloud picked up the bowl with the potion he had made earlier and walked over to where Kevin laid upon the ground.

"Keep him, still," he said.

Jade's heart pumped adrenaline to her limbs as she pushed down on Kevin's shoulders. "Hang in there, K. It will be over soon. I know you can hear me. You've got this." Jade didn't have much faith in her words, but she had a feeling in her heart... and a queasy sensation in her gut, though she didn't know whether it was a negative or positive intuitive sign. Thundercloud kneeled down and clasped Kevin's head between his knees. He picked up a thick branch from the array of herbs splayed out beside him and wedged it between Kevin's teeth. Jade watched as he moved with skilled precision. Thundercloud dribbled the liquid potion into Kevin's mouth and stroked his Adam's apple, encouraging him to swallow, then he held the young man's mouth closed, but liquid leaked from Kevin's nose. Chief Thundercloud opened K's mouth again and stroked his Adam's apple. Jade didn't think she could keep him still any longer. He was strong. He suddenly went rigid, so Thundercloud turned Kevin's head to the side, facing away from the fire. Easing his discomfort, Thundercloud was able to clear his airway, allowing Kevin to lay calmly again.

"Is he alive?" she asked as she laid her head on Kevin's chest. She could feel his heart beating and see his chest rising, but still, she needed to hear it from Chief Thundercloud. She was afraid.

"Yes. But the next few hours will tell us if he will live or die," Chief Thundercloud said. "He should sleep now.

Jade slid off Kevin and delicately arranged his hand under his head, while his other hand lay across his body. She moved his legs and torso into a recovery position, facing away from the fire.

"I will take care of your friend. You need to do the grouse dance. I don't mean stand up and turn around and point your head down to the ground like in the dance ceremonies. You need to create the spiral of energy with the drum and imagine the energy as a whirlpool or a tornado. Using the energy of the bear, go deep inside yourself and enter the spiral to the Dream Lodge to exit this realm and enter the Realm of Lost Souls. It will be desolate, and darker than an eclipse since it's the home of dark shadows. It will be choked with sorrow and gorged with pain. You will see oceans of tears and starless skies and you will hear hideous sounds. There are horrors I have only been told of by Great Turtle."

"Great Turtle has been to the Realm of Lost Souls?" Jade asked. "Yes. Pick up your drum and your wand. It's time for you to travel into the void. Do not linger there with thoughts of wonderment or you will be in limbo forever. You must be swift and pass through the void into the Realm of Lost Souls to find the missing part of your father's soul. When the missing piece of his soul is revealed to you, place it in your heart to keep it safe. Travel back with the energy of the sacred spiral, the dance of the sharp-tailed grouse. You will find it within the rhythm of the drum. When you return, stop drumming and race to your father and breathe into his chest. Breathe out the missing part of his soul until you have no air left in your body. Pray that the demon and its kind doesn't follow you and fight for the possession of your father's body and soul. If it does, we will have to join forces to banish it from your father and force it back to the world of the dead.

JADE HEARD THE AIR TRAVELING THROUGH THE FOX HOLE. SHE had no idea how she was going to do anything Chief Thundercloud expected of her. She must be in a nightmare. That's it! She's lying in bed and when she wakes she will find her mom and dad in the kitchen, laughing over a cup of coffee and burnt toast. Her eyes glazed over.

Chief Thundercloud yelled, "Raven Wings!"

She didn't want to listen. He was a figment of her imagination. He wasn't real. She was having a bad dream because of all the stories her great-grandmother had told her while growing up.

The spirit of Great Turtle appeared before her, holding Kevin's hand. "Please tell me he's not dead?" she asked Great Turtle.

"He is not dead. I will care for him, as his grandmother is doing, and all the spirits he has touched. He is in good hands, but you have to go now. Step into your future. No matter how dark it may seem. If you stay, you will wither and die, and so will the world around you. You need to grow and blossom into the person you are meant to be. You chose this journey long ago before you even walked upon this Earth. You are from Great Spirit, and one day you will understand." Her great-grandmother and Kevin fragmented into nothing; their spirits disappearing.

Jade wedged the wand down the front of her bra with the fluffy white grouse feathers facing upward. It was the closest place to her heart.

Chief Thundercloud gave her a handful of white sage leaves and said, "Chew on this. Do not swallow it, or spit it out, until I tell you to or you will become prey to spiritual squatters. Evil squatters."

She did as he instructed and then took the pouch and placed it on her father's chest. With her drum and healing rod, she sat at his head. "I'm coming for you," she said with determination and picked up her drum.

She looked at it lying in her lap and touched the deer-skin. A turquoise thread of peacefulness unraveled from her braid and found its way through her internal chaos. It radiated from the boundaries of her skin into her ethereal body. She made circles upon the surface of the deerskin with the drumstick. Listening to the soft sound it made, she tapped the drum in the middle. It resonated. She touched the drum again and began beating out a steady rhythm. Feeling calm, she lifted it from her lap and weaved her fingers around the waxed string. Jade held the drum in her right hand and drummed with her left. The vibrations washed over her as she remembered Great Turtle teaching her how to listen to the drum. She held the drum to her face and listened; it sounded like a deep voice chanting into a fan. She moved it to her left, and then to her right, and heard the whispers and felt the beat. It resonated within her soul.

Chief Thundercloud's voice, telling her to chew the sage and that it was time to open the doorway, was faint. Her energy harmonized with the drum... it was luminous, a moment that she would never forget. Her drumming became faster and faster; playing different parts of the drum, creating different sounds. She closed her eyes and this time, Chief Thundercloud didn't call her back. She felt her energy stretch out like a pair of wings and she soared into the spiral of energy pulsing from the drum. Flying with the wings of a raven was even better than Casey raising her off the ground and into the air. She was in control and had so much more freedom.

Enjoying the bliss of being a bird, Jade glided into the slipstream of the descending whirlpool of energy, searching the void. The air cooled as she entered a darker spiral, like a wormhole gone bad. Her circular movements through this space became slow. She was in a dense substance that seemed to be similar to water. It turned to sludge, sticking to her wings like oil. She was being dragged down like a sinking ship when something touched her leg. She listened for the drum again and fell into its rhythm, suddenly ascending this time, spiraling through the darkness out of the sludge. She allowed the water to propel her to the surface, where she gasped for air.

It was a moonless night. The waves rose and fell, jostling her between them like a gang of tormenting children. The rocking was physically sickening and she realized she was in an ocean of tears. Jade let the swell sweep her up to the crest of a wave and she quickly searched for land. There was nothing but blackness, thick as ink. The ocean dragged her down and up the next cresting wave and the next. Still, she saw nothing. The suction of the sea pulled her higher and higher, and dropped her suddenly. The darkness concealed the depth of the fall. She flailed her arms on her way down and tried to imagine the ocean calming, but the waves didn't stop. The sea was wild. She realized that she was going to drown, so she imagined a bright summer's day. She called out to the turtles to rise up from their sleepy depths to help her, but there were no turtles, no dolphins, and no fish. Whatever was in the murky water wouldn't be found on Earth. This place didn't belong in her world and she didn't belong in this world.

The water was icy cold and she shivered as the waves broke. She choked on the greasy, salty water that made up this ocean of tears. Her teeth were chattering. She had to get out and trust her instincts. Frantically, Jade swiveled, searching for any sign, or magnetic pull—a whisper from her father, or an ingrained knowing—some sort of sign. Something brushed past her leg. She flipped over and dove under the water getting away from the manic rock of the ocean's surface. Swimming in the black water was like standing in an airless darkroom. She had no idea if she was moving forward. Her head felt dizzy, lost spatial sense, rose to the surface and vomited.

Where is this place! She was going to die here. FUCK! At the top of her lungs, she screamed, "Dad! Dad!"

Keep it together. To expel energy because of exasperation will make me weak, physically, mentally, and emotionally. Jade swam madly, was lifted by another wave, and kept on swimming, smacking her head on something hard. Dazed, she reached out her hand. It felt like wood, so she slapped at it, feeling around for its edges. She held on while the ocean rocked her unmercifully. The plank of wood was wide enough for her to haul herself up and over the edge. The quartz on the end of the wand, nestled between her breasts, jabbed into her skin.

She looked down at the quartz crystal and thought she saw a glint of light. Everything was pitch black and it was freaking her out. She needed light. She sat on the piece of wood and stared hard at the quartz crystal until the light shone a little brighter. It was like a star traveling across the universe, becoming brighter and brighter until she could see her body again. She withdrew the wand from her clothing and held it high above her head as a beacon.

She thought that what she saw would give her nightmares forever.

A shipwreck: the planks of wood were from the carcass of an old sailing ship, the deck of which was covered in live dismembered body parts. They were searching for their counterparts. Heads with long messy hair floated in thin air. Known as Flying Heads, or Kanontsistonties; they were a cannibalistic creature from Great Turtle's nightmarish mythological stories. Carved into the wooden planks were faces of screaming children, the victims of Abiku, another evil spirit she had been told about by Great Turtle.

Jade shuffled into the middle of the joined planks of wood, careful not to lie on a child's screaming head as she sat up. Beyond the towering waves, partly hidden by shadows, were mountains. If there are mountains, there will be land. *Wow, state the obvious why don't you*, she muttered to herself. The sound of her voice was small in the haunted vastness.

Shivering from the cold, she searched above for a glimpse

of night sky. Gray cotton-candy clouds were streaming over-head. The clouds shifted into ghostly figures moving toward her. As the figures began to wail, the pitch quickly elevated into screeching and squelching and the demons tore through the air, getting closer. They sounded like hundreds of shrieking voices. The demons descended like moths racing to the brightness, as Jade cringed in physical pain. She needed to shut off the light.

The ocean rose up, lifting the wooden planks and Jade into the air toward the demons, while the wand, held high above her head, slipped from her hand. It was falling beyond the edge of her tiny platform. Jade stretched out her arm and body to catch it. Everything seemed to be in slow motion. The wand toppled into the ocean as Jade dived in after it. She dove, face first through the murky liquid after the wand inches from her grasp, she snatched it up and immediately secured it under her bra and clothing. She assumed its light would be hidden, so she swam underwater until it dimmed and the air in her lungs had expired.

She controlled herself from bursting out of the water. Her lungs were on fire, but she kept treading water just below the skin of the ocean. She looked up. With her mouth shut tight, afraid of swallowing someone's tears, she peeked above the waterline and breathed through her nose. Faint sounds of moaning and a pungent odor of sewage wafted over the ocean from her left. Jade free-styled toward the smell in search of a shoreline. She tried to remain undetected by the wailing ghosts. Every time she thought of them flying above, her anxiety escalated. It was easy to believe that, any minute, they would swoop and feed on her soul.

Jade clenched her jaw to stop her teeth chattering. She had to keep it together! At the top of each cresting wave, she searched for a glimpse of the mountain she thought she had seen earlier. Her neck was getting sore since she was holding her head as high as possible, so no water could enter her mouth. If she didn't find land soon, she would drown. The further she went, the stronger the smell became. She was tiring, her arms burning and heavy. The ocean was relentless, although she calculated that each time the wave scooped her up, it dropped her closer to shore. The waves were reducing in height and strength and the smell of decay became stronger. She desperately swam through the salty water.

Fatigue, worthlessness and pending doom filled her body and mind. Her efforts were hopeless. Raucous moaning was coming from the beach ahead and the sound fueled her anguish, then her feet hit bottom. The ocean floor didn't feel like sand; it was lumpy and hard like shards of rock, or perhaps a coral a reef. If she wasn't wearing shoes, her feet would have been sliced up. The exhaustion and agony in her arms multiplied when she stood and the cold air wrapped around her body. She half expected her shirt and cargos to turn as stiff as cardboard. The moaning and crying were coming from the beach. As Jade stumbled over the coral, she moved toward the shore and looked about for the demons, then drew out her crystal wand to light up the dark.

Upon the beach lay thousands of human bones, skulls, fleshy arms and legs, all scattered across the shoreline. Beyond the bones were people partly buried in different stages of decomposition and many were crying, pleading for someone to help them. Jade looked down into the water at her feet, but she wasn't walking on coral; she was walking on the bones of the dead. She had imagined the Realm of Lost Souls as misty and made of energy, not something as tangible as bones that crunched underfoot. There was nowhere else to go. She wanted to cry, she wanted to howl, and she wanted to scream aloud. This was an awful place. Her heart was thumping and banging in her chest, but she wished for the silence to return. With each step she raised her shoulders closer to her ears as if afflicted with pain. She just wanted to go home.

"Please forgive me for stepping on your bones. Sorry, Sorry," she said as she emerged from the ocean of tears.

Hundreds of dead people were beneath the sand and her feet. She formed a mental image of her dad, needing to visualize his smiling face because so much darkness was already pouring into her being.

An old man half buried in the sand, stretched out his only visible arm. "Please, can you help me?"

Jade remained silent. The man's hand touched her shoelace as she moved away.

"Please, I'm who you're looking for. You are my child, and I am yours. Quickly, take me. Take me now. Fold me within your heart and take me with you." The man continued to plead.

"You're not my father," Jade said to the face protruding from the sand.

"Yes, I am, come back here, child." "I'm not a child!"

"Then why are you sobbing like a worthless child?"

Jade hadn't realized she had started crying. Her wand was held high, casting shadows over countless bodies. She didn't want to see into their eyes, or their pleading faces, as she walked among them. As she passed between a decapitated head covered in seaweed, and a torso, a hand reached up out of the sand and grabbed her by the ankle.

"Hey, little lady. It's me, it's grandpa, have you come to take me home? Don't mind him," he said, tilting his head toward the other head covered in seaweed. "He won't bite. And they say seaweed's good for you. Ha, ha. What you crying for, lass?"

Jade shook her leg free.

"No need to be so violent!" the man said.

In the distance, she could hear a toddler sobbing and calling out, "Mama, mama."

"Mommy, dat you? Mommy, we go home? Come, we go home? Bottle mommy? Blankie, mommy, I cold."

Jade covered her ears, blocking out the maddening calls from the fragmented bodies and souls around her. She concentrated on her father's face.

"I'm here, over here."

She dropped her hands. Her healing wand lay idle by her

thigh. "Dad?" she whispered.

"This way. Over here."

Jade quickly moved toward the sound of her father's voice. A face protruding from the wet sand had beckoned her. Jade hesitated before pointing her wand down at the face to see the features. If it was her father, how was she going to get him out? Slowly, she lowered the wand. The face shied away from the light, blinking rapidly. "Yes, darling, it's me."

Her dad would never call her darling.

"Don't you recognize your dad? Help me out, will you? You'll see. Give ya daddy a kiss."

She didn't recognize the face. He sounded like her dad, but it wasn't him. Jade moved carefully, stepping between the bodies, avoiding the outstretched arms. There were so many lost souls. Beyond the sand was scrubland, but before advancing through it into the forest and up the mountain, she turned back and prayed. "God, Great Spirit, if you truly exist, which, at this point in time I'm assuming you do, please reach into the darkness and show mercy to these troubled souls. Scoop up the parts and make them whole again."

She wiped her face and turned to the mountain. She closed her eyes, summoning a memory of her father scraping burnt toast, the smell of it filtering through the house and her nostrils, and the stench of the beach was momentarily masked. She heard him whistling a tune she didn't know. She was about five and sitting on a kitchen chair, waiting for her breakfast of orange juice and toast. She was singing and humming a song about black oceans, tears and walking upon the bony backs of men, while flicking through a book about the Seven Wonders of the World.

"What is your favorite, Jade?" he had said with his back to her. "The Great Barrier Reef," she had responded.

"Why?"

"Because it's the rainforest of the ocean. And I love turtles and swimming in the ocean. What's your favorite thing, Daddy?"

He had put the plate of toast on the table in front of her. She'd picked up a triangle and licked off the butter speckled with charcoal before biting the toast.

"You! You are my favorite natural wonder in the world," he said, sipping his coffee and checking his watch.

"Why, Daddy?"

"Because when you're happy the sun shines, when you're sad the clouds gather, when you're miserable we get rain, and when you're angry we get wild storms. When you're thinking, I can hear the birds singing."

"Oh Daddy, you're silly," she had said, wiping her mouth with her napkin. "Shall we go now? I don't want to be late to great-gran's place."

"Don't sing that song any more, sweetie."

She remembered the feeling of his strong hands lifting her up out of the chair and planting her feet firmly on the floor. He had taken her hand, and she could almost feel her hand in his now.

Jade stepped into the scrub and slowly moved up the

mountain into the woods of sorrow, pushing back the branches, forging a pathway. The brush was so thick she couldn't even make out her feet. Suddenly the ground disappeared and there was nothing she could do to stop herself from stepping into empty space. She screamed as she plummeted down a dark shaft. The wand was tumbling ahead of her, its light rapidly diminishing. Jade fixed her eyes on the wand, afraid it would disappear. Her screams seemed to trail on forever. She hit the bottom, and her screams echoed up the shaft as she cried out in pain. She discovered her ankle was twisted at an odd angle when she tried to stand up, but spied the wand about six feet away. Terrified the light would go out, Jade gritted her teeth and shuffled awkwardly on her side, dragging her broken ankle, to fetch her wand. The clear quartz terminator's fluorescent radiance amplified as she touched it.

She felt like she was continuously falling down.

"Dad!" she screamed in despair. She curled up in a fetal position and whimpered, defeated. There was no way out, she couldn't walk, she couldn't climb.

She was as doomed as every other lost soul she walked among.

What had happened? Had she dropped the drumstick and stopped drumming? Had her heart stopped beating? Was Kevin okay? *He's probably dead. You both are.*

"Shut, the hell up!" she yelled into the darkness. Her own thoughts were driving her insane. For once she wished she had no thoughts and that her mind was only a blank.

10

J ade's throat was sore from screaming. She sniffed back tears and held the wand up, moving it around to see the extent of the shaft. The light touched the wall and she could see it was made from hundreds of skulls stacked on top of each other. What is it with this place, she thought, skulls are everywhere I go. The damp shaft was approximately eight feet wide. The situation looked hopeless.

I'm useless, why would anyone choose me for a spiritual quest. It's no game—her father's life was at stake. Jade didn't have the ability, or whatever it would take to find him. She figured she would die of starvation because of her broken ankle. And even if it wasn't broken, she still couldn't climb out of the shaft. She lay curled up on the floor, tightly wrapping her arms around her knees and sobbed.

Exhausted, she rested on the ground beside her wand.

The moisture on the right-hand side of the shaft was increasing. A dirty-red, thick mud, like dark blood, oozed out of the skulls' eye sockets in the walls. Jade shuffled into a sitting position and leaned against the opposite wall to get a better look. The burgundy mud was trickling down the wall and it became a steady flow that splashed at the bottom of the shaft. It soon turned into a stream, gushing like someone had turned on a faucet—red mud pooling on the ground. Skulls dislodged and dropped into her lap. Jade backed away from the bleeding wall. "*Shit!*" She scrabbled to her feet, all her weight on the one good leg. Skulls continued to be dislodged by the pressure of the red mud and tumbled into the pool around her.

In a short time, the shaft would be flooded. Jade braced herself against the wall. She lost her balance and fell. As she tried to stand, Jade slipped and lost hold of her wand. The mud concealed its glow. The darkness was consuming. "No, no, no." On her knees, ignoring the pulsing pain in her ankle, Jade stuck her hands in the mud that now rose up past her elbows. She fumbled in the dark for her crystal wand, touched it and held on. It was slippery and hard to grip and she hit her ankle with the wand on the way up. Screaming in pain, she fell back into the slush. The raw emerald gemstone on the wand glowed, pulsating with light that snaked into the quartz crystal. The light was magnified, generating a beam, like a laser. Jade sat in burgundy mud that was now waist deep, and wiped muck off of herself. Quivering in pain, she pushed the quartz laser against her swollen ankle. The light grew brighter and penetrated her skin. Her veins bulged with blood and her ankle expanded like a softball before shrinking back to its normal size, pain-free. Jade looked at the wand and said, "Why didn't you do that sooner? Why didn't Chief Thundercloud tell me you could do that?" She waited for an answer that was not forthcoming.

The wall of skulls suddenly burst like the banks of a river; shards of bone hit her head and scratched her face. She closed her mouth and covered her head as the bloodied mud cascaded over her. The volume of sludge bore down on the opposite wall. Jade lashed out and punched a hole in the wall and it caved in, forming a tunnel for the crimson mud to stream into. She needed to stand, but the mud's force was too rough. Jade hooded her eyes and tried to see. She gave up and struggled to stand; the red mud was almost up to her neck. The avalanche of bones swirled around her, pouring out of the shaft, dragging her along. Feet first, she was sucked under and swept through the opening, sliding, descending rapidly. Flat on her back she raised her head out of the dirty, red stream and tried not to panic. She cleaned the mud from her eyes. The space was tight, the ceiling inches away, and the area was getting tighter.

She held the wand against her chest, keeping the tip of the crystal above the surface of the mud. It drove the darkness back and revealed the tightening of the channel to the point that she could see she was going to get stuck; terrified, she cried out for help. Her nose scraped against the ceiling as the mud covered her mouth, her face. She closed her eyes. Dad, I'm sorry, I've failed you.

The longest she had ever held her breath was for a little over three minutes. Her lungs were aching, as the flow of mud accelerated, and Jade was propelled out of what could have been a sewage pipe. In mid-air, she drew a deep hurried breath before she was dumped into a pool of slush. Jade fought her way to the surface and removed as much of the crap from her face as she could.

The crystal wand continued to glow with a brilliant white light. She held it high. On the far bank, a small slight figure was crouched beside some rocks. It looked like a little boy and it sounded as if he was crying. He was rocking back and forth. Jade, cautious, searched for a possible trap. She saw an archery target pictured in her mind. Did that mean she has found her target? Or does it mean she is the target? Whatever it is, she had to get to the far rocky shore. Jade swam through the warm mud, her breathing labored in the thickness of the slush. The crystal, now partly under the mud, was dull. Jade decided to stick it down her bra, worried she would drop it and never find it again. It would be terrible to be trapped forever down here. In the darkness, she moved toward the bank. She had the jitters, feeling as if someone was watching, or creeping up on her from behind. Turning reactively, she saw a set of orange eyes looking down on her. She pulled the crystal wand out from between her breasts and held it high, but nothing was there.

The bank was slippery and nearly impossible to climb so

she dug the healing rod into the muddy embankment and held on; she didn't want to slip back into the goo. Now looking at it clearly, she thought it looked more and more like iron-rich blood.

"Hello?" she said, shakily. Her voice was loud and echoed in the vast chamber. Jade searched for a vine to pull herself up. "Can you help me get up this embankment?" Jade was cagey, worried he was going to turn out to be the soul-sucking demon Chief Thundercloud had warned her about. Her skin crawled. The smell of whatever it was she was in, made her gag.

The boy didn't turn, but Jade thought she heard tutting and a slithering sound coming from above, past the hole she was ejected from. The sound was behind her and close to the ceiling … something shifted.

"I need your help. The mud's warm, but it's sticky and feels really yucky," Jade said to the boy.

"Shh, or he will eat your soul, and then he will eat mine too," the boy said in a whisper.

"If you don't help me, I'll scream, and then he will come? *Who is* 'he'?"

She could see the boy stop rocking and stand up. He looked up to the ceiling before running over on his little legs. He then stopped halfway, as if thinking about his choice to help her. Wearing denim jeans and an oversized, grubby white printed t-shirt, he looked like was around five years old. The image was of a bulked-up fly with square glasses, ready for action as if it was a superhero.

"Cool t-shirt, kid," Jade said.

His face was lined from tears. He stopped and looked down at his shirt, then ran his hand over the print. "It was my big brother's. He lets me wear it when I am scared." That explains why it looked too big for him.

"I'm scared. You're lucky to have a big brother willing to share with you. I don't have any brothers or sisters."

The boy walked closer. Jade held her emotions together, trying to stop the hopelessness from making a home inside her again, a side effect from this place. She wanted to go home more than anything, but she also wanted to get back to Kevin. *He's probably dead by now.* "My friend had a little brother, his name was Alex. He was powerful and clever. You remind me of him."

The boy looked up at the ceiling, then rushed over to her. He crouched down and looked at her. "He won't let me go home?" he said, and touched the wand.

She was afraid he was going to take it and leave her stuck in the mud. *It's just an old stick, that's all it is.* "You can come home with me. Alex's big brother is sick. He is waiting for me to return, so we can get him medicine. Otherwise he'll die. I'll hold on to this old stick." And as soon as she said it, the wand appeared to be nothing more than a stick pulled from a fire that still had a faint glowing tip. The boy noticed the wand had changed and stepped back.

"Hey, how did you do that?" he shouted. He quickly clapped his hands over his mouth.

"Give me your hand and I'll tell you. Maybe you're not as

strong as Alex. Maybe you can't help me? That's okay." Jade pretended to slip back into the mud.

"Yes, I am." Reluctantly, he reached out with his chubby little hand and took her hand in his. Jade pulled on the wand, thrusting herself up and slithered onto flat ground like a seal, then grabbed the wand from the mud.

The boy ran back to where he'd come from. Jade crouched low and followed him. "What's your name?" she whispered, crouching and scraping off the crimson mud.

"You have to go now."

"Come with me," said Jade.

"No, he won't let me go."

"Who won't let you go? What's your name?"

"Why do you want to know my name? You're not my friend, you tricked me."

"I didn't trick you. How did I trick you?"

"You made that sparkling magic wand turn into an ordinary stick." "Yes, I did. I was afraid you would steal it from me. If you took it, I would be left in the dark, and it's very dark and scary here."

"That's not mud," the boy said. "It's blood. It's the blood from the people that he brings here. He sucks out this magical stuff from the body and then squeezes out the blood. It's horrible, but he wants me to see. The people look like they have no juice left, like old plums, just squishy-squashy. And he chews on the bones. But he loves the blood and saves some for later for his sleeping family. The magical stuff has to be taken first; he likes that the most."

"What family? There are others?" Jade asked in a rush.

"I don't know," the boy said. "I hide in there." He pointed to a small hole. "It can't get me in there."

"Have you seen any others?" Jade asked.

"I sometimes come out when it's sleeping. I saw his family sleeping. He has lots of family. Up there." He pointed to the ceiling and the walls from where she came.

"My name is Jade. What's yours?" Jade pushed down the rising panic.

"You've got a kind face, Jade. My name is Kayden Scott Freeman. Can you stay with me and protect me with your magic stick?"

Jade felt something touch the back of her neck and she quivered. Her father's name was Scott Freeman. Kayden was his younger brother's name. Kayden died at the age of five. Her dad had told her the sad story of his death. When her dad was a teenager, he got caught up with the wrong crowd. One afternoon, he was supposed to pick Kayden up from kindergarten, but he forgot and went to the mall with his friends. Kayden had walked home alone and while crossing the road he was hit by a car.

Jade grabbed the boy's face and stared into his wide eyes. He looked frightened and angry at her sudden movement. Her dad's eyes were glaring back at her. *This is her dad*. Why would he say his name was Kayden? Probably because he carries the guilt for his little brother's death.

"Your name is Scott. You're Kayden's big brother." The little boy's eyes filled with sorrow. "No, my name is Kayden.

My big brother was Scott. He died a long, long time ago. He was so sad. I kept talking to him, but he couldn't hear me."

"Kayden, I think you're Scott. I think you're confused because you miss Kayden so much. Scott grew up to be a handsome man. He went to university and met a beautiful woman named Ellen. They fell in love."

"Ellen," the little boy said, confused. Something shifted in the boy's eyes. A light glowed around him. "Ellen."

Jade stood back and watched the boy's face age. He had an expression of someone much older.

"Ellen," he said in a mature voice. "I can take you to Ellen," Jade said.

Overhead, something much bigger than her swooped down at them, transforming into a two-legged creature. She had seen this demon somewhere before. Its skin was slippery and it looked like a melting candle. It was snarling like a rabid dog with rows of sharp yellow teeth receding down into its throat. Hot, pungent breath escaped from its mouth, the same stench as the crimson mud. Its eyes were orange. Jade protectively reached her hand behind her to conceal Kayden and her wand touched his chest. She felt the impact of his soul as the boy's ethereal light wormed its way through her back and into her heart.

The demon hadn't fully transformed into its new form and Jade got the sense that it was weak. That's why it wanted the boy, her dad. Her dad's inner child was the final piece required for the demon to claim a living body and return permanently to the realms of Earth. Her dad's inner child had been hiding inside his dead brother, Kayden. The creature needed her dad's soul to take full control of his body. That would mean that the demon would look like a man, it would inhabit her dad's body, and it would be free to do as it pleased *on Earth*. But it had chosen the wrong person; she would fight for her father. She would fight, even if it meant that she fought until her dying breath. Jade would not let this creature claim her father's soul, or body.

The demon reached out its claw-like hands with its long, pointed, dirty fingernails, and Jade lashed out with her wand, hitting its upper body and arms. She reached for her bowie knife while it wrapped its long fingernails around the boy's neck, drew him close, and sniffed.

Jade jostled with the creature trying to pry its fingers off the boy's throat. She flinched, cutting herself on one of the demon's sharp nails. She pulled her knife free and stabbed at it. The creature dropped the boy and pulled back from her, but it wasn't fazed by the stab wounds and gashes she inflicted. Her blood dripped from what appeared to be its finger. Sniffing at the blood, it turned to acid, burning the creature. Jade perked up after seeing the fear well up in the demon's orange eyes. It was scared of her blood. Quickly, it tore off what looked to be a long fingernail and tossed it aside.

As the creature picked up the boy's lifeless body, she felt confident the body was just a shell and its true essence, her dad, was safe inside her. With the knife, she stabbed at it before it leaped into the air and out of sight.

11

Jade let the creature have the body. She wasn't going to chase it, but she needed to find a way out. She had what she came for, which was her dad, safely tucked away, spiritually embedded inside her heart. But where was the way out? Jade looked at the dark pool of blood—she didn't want to dive back in there, but there didn't seem to be any other way. She felt a tremor under her feet and the faint sound of distant drum beats entered her consciousness. Jade started to run to the rhythm, touching the clay walls, trying to find an opening, a door, a window, a place to hide, anything. The creature gave out a frustrated cry; it must have realized the soul was no longer attached to the boy's body. She could hear a clicking, a flapping of wings. She had never been a fast runner, and today was no different. There was always a point when she would trip over her own feet. As she ran, Jade sensed she had reached top speed. She was going to topple over at any second, or be scooped up by the creature's talons and then it was game over.

If only Kevin was here. He could open up a doorway marked 'exit'. She needed to get back to him. Jade concentrated hard on Kevin, imagining she was running toward him. It was useless though; he was in a coma or he might be dead already. No, she had to stop thinking of him as dead. Jade was ready to give up, but knew she had to keep going or this terrible place would become her tomb. It was up to her to finish this.

The walls appeared to vibrate and wobble, as if they weren't even real. But she felt the coldness and the solidity under her hand. Jade looked back at the dirty-red mud. Right now it was real, it was all too real and there was nowhere else to go. The surface rippled with each beat of the drum. With her wand held out in front, Jade dived into the bloody mud, spearing the layers, penetrating its depths. She held her breath and swam down. It was so illogical to escape from a soul-sucking demon by diving into a warm pool of blood, but what was logical about any of this! The blood thinned as Jade continued down, feeling like she could be a cell zooming through a pulsating vein.

With her eyes squeezed tight, Jade visualized swimming to the bottom of a turquoise blue ocean, swimming to where the turtles would be. She imagined Great Turtle, Kevin, everyone she knew smiling and having fun. As Jade heard the sounds of her mom and dad laughing, the crimson mud thinned out even more and it became easier to swim. She could feel it turning to water around her body. The oscillations of the drum slowed to a steady pace and the water spiraled around her. She stopped swimming down and turned upward, allowing the force of the spiraling energy to quickly draw her up to the surface. She drove upward, her lungs ready to burst. Her head throbbed; she couldn't distinguish between the drum and the throbbing of her cranium. She breached the surface and gasped, a rush of air filled her lungs and the sun kissed her face.

Jade felt the warmth of a fire against her stiff body. The taste of blood and the smell of sage rushed to her throat. The fragrance of freshly ground herbs flushed her olfactory system. She was back in the cave and she was still drumming. Back with Chief Thundercloud, her dad, and Kevin. Between the beats, she could hear the soft baritone chants of Chief Thundercloud's soothing voice. Her wrist was hurting, but still, she didn't stop drumming. The closer she settled down into her body, the more aware she became of how stiff she was. She was going to hurt tomorrow. Out of breath as if she had run a marathon, she could smell her own perspiration. Her coccyx and every other bone in her body screamed for her to move and stand up. Jade opened her eyes, but she still didn't have control over her entire being. Chief Thundercloud stopped chanting.

"Go slow Raven Wings, but you must hurry." *How do you go slow and hurry at the same time?* She felt the urgency, but also knew she had to go slow, because her spirit hadn't finished nestling into her own skin, and she wasn't alone. She had a hitchhiker. Lethargic, she stretched out her legs that were riddled with pins and needles. It was a struggle to sustain a steady drumbeat while folding her numb legs to kneel. She leaned over her father's body and abruptly ended drumming. She dropped the drum beside her, and with force, she blows intensely onto his chest, breathing out a channel of light, allowing his spirit to be reconnected to his heart. She continued breathing out until she had no breath left.

Chief Thundercloud reached out a bowl to her and said, "Spit."

After Jade spat the sage into the bowl, Thundercloud threw it into the fire, which exploded as if it had been doused with gasoline. Jade blows onto her dad's chest again, creating a stronger connection between his spirit and his heart. A channel of violet filled his chest. Six more times Jade breathed light into her dad's chest and each breath contained a different color: indigo, sky-blue, emerald-green, yellow, orange, and red. And each color filled one of his seven energy centers throughout his body, from his crown to his base chakra. Her breath shortened. Under her hand, his heartbeat strengthened.

Chief Thundercloud handed her a bowl with a potion and said, "Rinse and spit." He pointed to the fire.

She swirled the liquid around the inside of her mouth, then spat it over the fire. Again the flames exploded into life.

"Finish!" he said.

Jade saw stars, ready to pass out. She breathed one more time into her father's chest. Her face and his chest were illuminated with golden light. The ethereal casing that had protected the missing part of her dad's soul and wormed its way into her heart, had been completely returned to him through the ritual. Jade leaned back on her heels, waiting for something to happen—a deep breath, perhaps the twitch of an eye, anything. The colored vapors of light from the ethereal body dimmed. Waiting for him to wake, she glanced over her shoulder to see how Kevin fared.

"Oh, my god, will one of you wake up?" Jade yelled, exasperated. "Chief Thundercloud, why isn't my father waking up?"

Before Thundercloud could answer, her father's body started to convulse. His face was changing at high speed, transforming from his to that of the creature she faced in the Realm of Lost Souls. His whole body started to change and her father and the creature were fighting for control. For a few seconds, she thought the demon would be victorious as it continued to hold its form.

"What do I do?" Jade didn't like her dad's chances.

Chief Thundercloud chanted. Jade imagined he was calling on Great Spirit to help her dad. She struggled to think of what she could do. Grabbing her pouch, which had fallen to the ground, she wanted to lay the gemstones over his heart and the snake's vertebra over his throat, but there was no way she could do that if she couldn't keep him still. Jade threw herself onto her father's thrashing body.

Holding on to his arms, she yelled, "Dad! Fight! Dad, you can do this. Do it for Kayden. Do it for mom. You've got to fight it. Open your eyes. Look at me!"

His eyes flew open and they were orange. The demon's mouth full of sharpened teeth, sneered at her. It drew its lips back in an ugly smile, and she saw at least three rows of teeth. Its throat looked like teeth. The thrashing started again, then her dad's face was back. She turned away, burying her face in his chest, knowing how hard his struggle to maintain control was. Her finger was still bleeding, staining his shirt. Jade remembered what happened in the cave when she cut her hand on the demon's fingernail. It turned to acid and the demon recoiled in fear.

"Chief, help me open his mouth," Jade yelled. "Hold it open."

Jade opened the cut in her hand with the tip of her bowie knife until her blood flowed. Bracing herself for the pain, she rammed her hand into her dad's mouth.

"Feed on this!" She squeezed the blood from her hand.

The demon bucked her loose, launching her toward the fire. Her foot and lower leg landed in the flames, her pants catching alight. Jade smacked and patted out the flames and her pants shouldered as she rushed back to her dad. His body was twitching violently as the demon attempted to separate itself from his body, trying to escape. It was panicking. It became smaller, shriveling into an entity with wings. It fluttered above her dad's chest as if chained and pulled itself free, flying too close to the fire. The fire burst into manic black flames that smelled of burning rubber. Chief Thundercloud drank the last drop of potion in the bowl and as the severely deformed demon flew away from the fire, he sprayed the potion from his mouth, forming a glittering web that trapped the entity, making it drop to the ground and burst into a cloud of dust.

"Dad!" Jade went to her father, expecting him to be conscious, but still he didn't move. Each one of his energy centers began to open up like flowers. The light contained within each energy center flowed into his aura and surrounded him, looking like mystical vapors. Jade willed him to open his eyes, afraid they were going to be orange.

"There isn't anything else you can do, Raven Wings. He will need to wake slowly. He is weak, and the battle with the demon has put a strain on his body and heart."

"How long will we have to wait?" Jade said. "He'll wake, or perish."

"But his eyes were just open," Jade said.

"That wasn't your father's doing, it was the demon."

Jade lay with her head against her father's chest. "What about Kevin?"

"His fever has broken; he will come around in a few hours." "Come, Raven Wings. Clean yourself." He handed her the basin and soap. "Then sit with me by the fire," he said, removing a black cloth from his bag.

It felt good to scrub the drying blood from her arms and face. She rinsed her wand and bowie knife too, before dousing herself with the water from head to toe. On her way to sit by Chief Thundercloud, who was mixing herbs in his mortar, Jade kissed her dad on the cheek. She then checked on Kevin. Pushing the hair away from his eyes, she noticed his brow was clammy. She didn't understand what Chief Thundercloud had done to heal Kevin, but it was something that she wanted to learn.

Sitting back down next to Chief Thundercloud, he showed her how to cleanse herself, her wand and drum of negative energies by smudging and giving thanks to Great Spirit. He talked about the special cosmic opening and the wisdom available.

"Humanity may have fallen from grace, but it's a blessing. We must fall to rise, like the phoenix. It means that all of humanity is closer to ascending to the fifth dimension."

He explained how the wand would reveal its power in stages, just as she grows and develops in stages as a spiritual warrior and healer. He showed her how to make the antiseptic ointment for Kevin's wounds, and the rituals of cleansing the internal body to be spiritually worthy of the soul and its journey. There was so much more she would need to learn to honor the old ways and travel through the different realms.

The wand, in particular, was fascinating. After a few minutes of laser-like focus on the tip of the wand's clear quartz crystal, she was able to slip through one of its facets and travel to a place among the stars that was neither hot nor cold, where the entire surface was reflective. Crystal, geometric pastel-colored buildings reached to the skyline—a city. No other element was visible. She drew closer to the ground, which was different shades of green agate, and very beautiful. She touched it. It was warm. Her eyes took in a transparent skyscraper with seven sides, which would look like a star from space. The building next to it was long and was towering above some smaller, simpler shapes. She walked down the street and stood at a crossroads where there was an aquamarine pyramid.

There were no doors, no windows, no smog, and no people. She didn't even know if she was in the future, the past, or in an illusion. It felt authentic. If it was, she was sure it wasn't a place on Earth. Maybe she was even in a different slice of the universe. She should go back; with a single thought, she returned to her body.

Jade thought about Kevin and the portals he could create and how she could join him in discovering the secrets of Athanasia. But her journeys would be solo, she couldn't take anyone with her. Jade completed the merge into her body a lot quicker than her previous out-of-body experience. She was exhilarated, energized, and understood why Sophia meditated so much; it could quickly become an obsession.

Hours had now passed, and all the herbal tea had filled her bladder. She walked down a passageway until she found a spot to relieve herself, noticing that her usual level of anxiety was non-existent. The effects of the wand and its inter-dimensional travel could become addictive. A sense of calm she couldn't recall knowing before entering the portal membrane, had accompanied her since the journey through the crystal. Nothing made sense to her logically, but she was going to dismiss logic for now because what she felt was very real.

Another hour had gone by with Jade checking her dad and Kevin's progress every ten minutes. Her dad's breathing had deepened, and there were unstressed occasional movements under his eyelids and Kevin was sleeping peacefully. She had a strong urge to kick his foot to make him wake up!

"It's time to place the mark of the raven upon your skin," Chief Thundercloud said, picking up a parcel wrapped in black cloth. "Show me your wrist."

Jade moved away from Kevin and perched herself in front of Chief Thundercloud, offering her left hand.

"No, your other wrist," he said.

"What's wrong with my left hand? I'm left-handed."

"Nothing is wrong with your left hand. It goes on the right wrist, because healing energy from Great Spirit enters on the left and we share the energy from the right side."

"Input and output, like the flow of an electrical current," Jade said.

"Receiving energy and giving energy. You can also give from the left and the right simultaneously, but then you will receive the energy from here, or here," he said, touching her solar plexus and head. It depends on the type of energy you are channeling.

Chief Thundercloud unwrapped the black cloth revealing a sharpened bone and a small black bottle. He cleaned her wrist with one of his herbal mixtures and opened his bottle of ink. The heat from the fire was making her hot, or it could be the sight of the sharpened bone and the number of germs that could be on it. He dipped the tip of the bone into the bottle. Jade didn't like needles, but she zeroed in on Kevin and her dad to distract herself, recalling her journey through the Realm of Lost Souls. After a hundred or more picks and plucks at her skin, she looked back and saw he had created a beautiful tattoo. It had taken him an hour to draw and color a black raven in flight, with a star in front of its beak as if the star guided the bird. He then applied the ointment that she had originally made for Kevin, to her tattoo. It was an antiseptic and would help her arm to heal. Jade knew there would be no need for ointments once Kevin opened the portal for them to return home. If he would just wake up, she could place her dad in a bed back at Black Mountain. He would at least be comfortable.

Chief Thundercloud blew smoke in her face and said, "The spirit of the raven, turtle, sharp-tailed grouse, snake, deer, bear, and eagle, the medicine drum and the crystals on your healing wand, are within you. Your teacher will find you when you are ready. His name will be Gray Wolf and he will teach you the ways of the ancestors. His knowledge is vast, even greater than some of the ancestors of this world. He is of a lost tribe that came from the stars and he too, is from Great Spirit. He will teach you how to banish the spiritual demons that have begun to re-emerge and haunt this new world. You must expunge them until they are gone. Then we will all be free, no longer chained to this dimension. Humanity will rise to the fifth dimension." He paused and watched her face for a reaction before continuing his long-winded explanation.

"You no longer need to seek the past. You will no longer desire to correct the past. Give your attention to the future. Ascension to the fifth dimension cannot be undertaken until the evil is pushed back into the realms from whence they came."

"But what I don't understand," said Jade, "is why these demons are still haunting humankind? We returned the Emerald Tablet, didn't we?"

"Before the gate was sealed, demons, evil and malicious spirits were trapped in the void. They have access to this world and they are searching for a way to remain, forever. The whiteout temporarily concealed the world from them, but we cannot live in a whiteout forever. You are ready. You proved yourself worthy by traveling through the void to the Realm of Lost Souls where you retrieved a most valuable part of your father's soul and fully restored him back to this Earth. You banished one demon, and with the help of your friends, you will destroy many more."

"How will I know my teacher?" Jade asked, so many questions swirled around in her brain.

"He and his kind are extraordinary and have abilities, like you and your friends do. Gray Wolf, among many things, is a shape-shifter. He could appear to you in many forms. He is a little like your friend Sophia. If she wanted to, she could stand here in spirit and join our conversation. Gray Wolf, too, can be the fly on the wall, but he can also do much more because he understands the medicines of Great Spirit, he knows the dance of the grouse and he knows the language of the stars. You and your friends must become masters and enable humankind's ascension to the fifth dimension."

"Where's the fifth dimension?" Jade halted him to ask another question.

"Through the crystal, you will be able to travel to the stars, go to other dimensions and converse with the future. Look up to the stars. It is where you've come from," Thunder-cloud said.

"I don't understand everything that you say. How can I come from the stars? There isn't any sign of life among the stars." She was growing confused again.

"Raven Wings, you are intelligent, you have scientific understanding. I know you're focusing on quantum physics, multiverses, and time travel. I, too, have studied at college and university and hide my fear behind knowledge. But the answers lie within you. You will try to find scientific theories to explain what your soul already knows. You must also listen to your heart."

"But, Chief Thundercloud, how will I find my teacher? I want to learn." She asked greedily.

"He will find you, but if you are not ready, he will not tell you that he is your teacher." Thundercloud held his finger up in warning.

"He sounds like he would be a very old, wise person. Can you tell me about my bracelet? I've seen it glow, and I've seen the markings rise and spiral in the air." Jade changed the conversation as she peered down at her bracelet in wonderment.

"It's made of copper. Copper is a transmitter. It contains the secret language of the stars, and it gives you great power, as it gave to Great Turtle. But once she learned the old ways, she no longer needed the power of the bracelet and left it for you."

Before she could ask any more questions, they heard her father stir. Chief Thundercloud put away his tools, while Jade went to her dad. His hand moved, tightening into a fist. There was eye motion behind his eyelids and his long black lashes, ones just like hers, blinked as he slowly opened them and gazed around. He seemed at a loss for words.

"Jade." He choked, his throat sounding dry. "Don't try to speak," Chief Thundercloud said. "Great Turtle's descendant has done well. You should be proud."

Jade hugged her dad so tight, she had to quickly let go for fear of hurting him. He was very fragile and his face, gray and gaunt. She helped him to a sitting position and gave him water to sip.

"Who's that?" he said slowly.

Jade looked over at Kevin. "He's my friend."

Her dad coughed, choking on the water. "What's wrong with him?" her dad asked, clearing his throat.

"Vampire bats," Jade said. "Do you remember what happened to you? You've been in a coma." She informed him gently.

"I'm not sure," he said, putting the bowl of water down.

"Let your father collect his senses, Raven Wings," Chief Thundercloud instructed her.

12

Chief Thundercloud proceeded to burn sage over his body fanning the smoke to spiritually cleanse her dad. He was now sitting up and had a colorful blanket made of light wrapped around him. She stared, fascinated, and thought about crystal buildings and prisms and Newtonian theories, while sipping the warm tea that Chief Thundercloud had made for her and her father.

"Earth to Jade," Kevin said in a soft voice.

He had propped himself up with one arm and was looking weak and shaky. Jade's heart fluttered. She was moved more than she wanted to admit, but she smiled at Kevin and he managed a small smile back. She thought about how they were going to have to crawl out through the fox tunnel and den and she couldn't envision him having enough strength to generate a portal back to the campsite.

Actually, she couldn't see him being able to do anything for a while.

"You did it. Didn't you?" he said, and his smile turned into a weak smirk.

"Are you going to introduce us?" her dad asked.

Jade, resting on her knees, rubbed the sudden sweat from her hands. "This is Kevin. He almost sacrificed his life to help me find you. He saved my life on more than one occasion. Dad, meet Kevin. Kevin, meet Dad," Jade said nervously.

"You're Callie's boy," her dad said.

They both could hardly move, but made great efforts to shake each other's limp hands.

Chief Thundercloud handed Kevin a bowl of tea and said, "Welcome, Kevin, to the land of the living dead."

"Pardon," Kevin said, dazed. Jade, too, was confused.

"Raven Wings, you should rest while these two find their legs," Chief Thundercloud said. "You will need your strength to crawl through the tunnel and help your father walk out of the forest. Your mother is anxious and waits for you at the cabins. You need to go to her; but first, I have one more thing to say, Raven Wings."

Jade searched his face intently, not knowing if she had the strength or emotional capacity to take in anything else.

"You have much work to do, Raven Wings. You, and your friends, are joined like a spiritual septagram, each a point of one seven pointed spiritual star. You are a gift from the creator. You are destined to cleanse this new world, and return the living to the creator in heaven among the Seven

Sisters that sit high above the Devil's Tower. Great Turtle foretold these days, and she honored me with the vision of her sight." He appeared grateful.

Kevin shuffled and crawled over to sit between Jade and Thunder- cloud. Chief Thundercloud handed her the ointment for Kevin's scratches and explained how best to apply the cream. In pain, Kevin lifted his shirt slowly. Jade, as gently as possible, applied the ointment. His skin felt warm, but the deep gashes had begun to heal, thankfully. She noticed tiny rows of dark brown sutures. Jade looked up at Thundercloud. "Are they what I think they are?"

"What do you think they are?" Chief Thundercloud said. Kevin was twisting to see his scratches.

"Keep still," Jade said to Kevin.

"Mandibles?" Jade's dark eyebrows rose in question and astonishment.

"Yes," Chief Thundercloud said, pointing to the trail of ants moving up the cave wall and into a hole.

"Army ants!" said Kevin shocked. "The wound will get infected, and I'll end up with sepsis," he said in a high-pitched register.

"Let me check your head." Jade said, getting up on her knees. 'Ants' biomaterials can be used for healing because their mandibles, in the past, have been used as sutures. And they have done a very nice job of sealing your wounds."

"What!" Kevin said startled.

"Stop being a baby," Jade said, gently tilting his head so she could see what Chief Thundercloud had done. "Besides the fact that you have ant claw marks in your head, the wounds look pretty clean."

"You're enjoying this, aren't you?" Kevin whispered to Jade.

"You must learn the old ways, Raven Wings. The world has changed."

Kevin relaxed, tolerating Jade's light touch as she smeared the ointment on his wounds. She saw him half smile at her dad.

"Has she always been this bossy?" Kevin asked in jest.

Her dad smiled at Jade, then at Kevin. "She is just like her mother, full of passion and determination. She doesn't mean to be bossy."

"Do you mind not talking as if I'm not here? As soon as you two are finished feeling sorry for yourselves..." She trailed off as her dad started to speak.

"And she has a tongue that can sting," her dad said.

Jade finished with the ointment and put it in Kevin's backpack along with her medicine pouch. She didn't want to share it with anyone just yet.

"It is so good to have you back, Dad. Wait till mom sees you." Jade hugged his arm. She closed her eyes for a moment and had a sudden jolt as pictures of the pool of blood, the cave, and demon's teeth and claws flashed into her mind. She shivered. The memories rushed back into her mind, terrorizing her for a few seconds.

"What's wrong?" her dad asked. "Nothing," she said, letting go of his arm.

Kevin had his eyes fixed on hers; she knew he was aware something happened that had scared her. She's going to have nightmares long after the memories had ostensibly faded. *Both of us are*, she mused, thinking of Kevin.

"Chief Thundercloud, what did you mean about 'land of the living dead'?" she asked.

Chief Thundercloud sat next to Kevin, completing a circle around the fire. He cast his eyes down before tilting his head to the ceiling. Closing them, he spoke in his native tongue, which none of them understood.

He opened his eyes and said, "Scott and Kevin, you should know that many creatures belonging to the angry gods of darkness will destroy what is left of this world if we do not destroy them first. The horrid men banished to the underworld, the evil demons and spirits of the shadows, madness, rage, sealed within the negative realms, were released seven months ago and will destroy what we have left, and prevent what is left of humanity from returning to our rightful place in the heavens. Once they become aware they can freely enter this world, nothing can stop them from finding a doorway. Not even the wrath of the Great Spirit can stop them. I'm sorry if I keep saying these things, but it is very important."

"But we closed the gate to hell and the negative realms and the underworld," Kevin said.

"They had already been released before the door was closed," Chief Thundercloud corrected, looking apologetic.

"How do you know all this?" Kevin asked. "The same way you know what's coming."

Jade didn't know where to look or how to feel. The joy and excitement of finding her dad was replaced with fear. A mountain of despair pressed down on her. Her head started to spin and she could feel her cheeks going cold.

"No, Raven Wings. No more, you must center your emotions. It's time to face your future. Can you not see what you have just done? You have defeated one of the darkest of creatures. And you are not alone, you have six friends. Together you will protect this realm."

"But this is supposed to be heaven on Earth now, this is supposed to be a new beginning," Kevin said.

"It is a new beginning, just not the one we imagined," Jade said.

Jade called on her memory of the movement of the trees and grounded her energy, sending her fear from her head down her body and her legs into the ground.

"So that means things can get better, right? We can maybe one day have a utopian world?" Kevin asked. "How long will this last? How many beasts will we need to slay, or send back to the negative realms?"

"How long is a piece of string?" said Chief Thundercloud.

Jade's dad seemed perplexed. He pulled her in close. "Wait a minute. She's only sixteen. How are these children going to defeat the monsters you speak of?"

"They are not children," Chief Thundercloud said to her dad. "Raven Wings is not just of your blood. She is of the blood of Great Spirit. She is our healer and warrior. They all are."

"It doesn't make sense," Jade said. "This is my father."

"Yes, but the light of Great Spirit is within you. You are a healer and warrior; you must take action like a warrior," Chief Thundercloud said. "You must stop hiding from yourself." He stood up and walked to the shelf and took down the rectangular box covered in shells, and handed it to her. It had a sliding lid. "Don't open it until you are alone and undisturbed."

"What's inside?" Jade said. She could tell by the way he continued to collect his things that he didn't want to answer any more of her questions.

"Your memories," said Chief Thundercloud finally.

"Maybe it's time to leave," Kevin said. "Let's find your mom and then head to the estate and talk with Casey, Sophia, and Tim. We might have to call Shaun and Rachel back, too." He moved as if uncomfortable.

"My memories?" Jade asked.

Her dad reached for the box. "Maybe I should hang on to that."

Jade ignored him and looked at Chief Thundercloud. "Thank you for keeping them safe. You should come with us," Jade said.

"I must stay here and find my son and his family. If I am confronted with something from the negative realms that I am unable to defeat, I will be calling upon you and your fellow warriors, Raven Wings," Chief Thundercloud said, gathering up his things. "It's time for me to leave." He handed Jade a bag of plants and a crocheted bag. "This is for your drum." Jade slid the drum into the bag and put it over her back. It felt like it belonged. "Thank you. Thank you for everything." She hugged him. "Your family. I almost forgot, they were seen heading to the Devil's Tower," Jade blurted out.

Chief Thundercloud nodded in thought. "This is great news. Thank you."

Her dad stepped forward and embraced Chief Thundercloud. "Thank you for taking care of me. I would have died if you hadn't come for me. Thank you."

Jade's wand was digging into her ribs. She pulled it out, and it lit up. Her father was standing by her side, but Kevin was alone on the other side of the fire.

"Where did you get that from?" Kevin said, struggling to stand up. "And when did you get a tattoo?" Her father challenged.

Jade grinned and looked at both of them. "I got the tattoo while you both were sleeping."

"And your mother knows of this?" her dad asked quizzically.

"K, are you strong enough to get us out of here?" Jade asked, changing the subject.

Kevin stood in front of Jade and her dad. He took their hands. "Yes. Okay, Mr. Freeman, you're going to feel a little queasy for a few seconds, but after that you're going to feel like brand new. I promise."

"Call me Scott."

Kevin stood between Jade and her dad. She watched in admiration as he created a well-formed doorway, a portal back to her mom at the Black Mountain campground. The membrane was scintillating, firing with sparks of light.

"What the hell?" her dad said. He let go of Kevin's hand. "Hey, where did it go?"

"Because you let go of his hand, the image evaporated from your perspective. It's still there."

Kevin grabbed Scott's hand again, and it reappeared. "You're getting really good at this, K," Jade said. "What is this?" her dad asked.

"We'll explain later, Mr. Freeman."

"Scott please," he said, leaning forward to peek into the portal.

"Okay, Scott. We'll step forward together. Don't let go of us. I don't want to leave you behind," Kevin said assuredly.

Jade quickly hugged Chief Thundercloud and again said, "Come with us?" The chief didn't answer, just hugged her back. Jade moved next to her dad, and he gave her a reassuring smile. On Kevin's command, they stepped forward. The bliss of the membrane was magical, and she could hear her father's thoughts and feelings of pure joy.

KEVIN OPENED A PORTAL TO THE PLACE IN THE FOREST WHERE they had met Russell and his sons. It seemed so long ago.

As they walked into the campground, people were working the crops, practicing shooting and archery. The few children were laughing and playing tag. One boy of around eight bumped into Jade. He stopped and stared at her for a second before running off. She wondered what the college, now campground, must have been like before the virus and thought to ask her mom and dad why they never came back here for a holiday.

Her mom was standing among a cluster of adults who were having a serious discussion. Jade, her dad, and Kevin, stepped out of the portal opening and headed toward the group. Her mom looked up and saw her, and Jade felt her dad tense at the sight of her mom.

"Ellen," he said. Tears pooled in his eyes, and he squeezed his lips together.

Her mom jogged across the open lawn, smiling at them all. But her eyes were fixed on her husband, Scott. She couldn't get to him fast enough, it seemed.

Within seconds Jade's mom and dad were embracing like long-lost lovers. Her mom pulled back as if to check it was really him. He had changed; he was scrawny and needed to put on a lot of weight. Satisfied it was him, her mom hugged him so tight, Jade thought this time his bones would surely snap under the pressure. Her mom let go and placed a hand on her chest, suppressing her obviously overwhelming emotions, then stretched out her arms and embraced them all.

"Where have you been? You're so thin, Scott. What

happened?" Ellen asked through a rambling of tears.

'I was on death's doorstep before I stepped into Kevin's portal.

Have you seen it, Ellen? It's marvelous."

"Yes, it's beyond my general scientific comprehension, but I have a theory," Ellen said, hugging Kevin.

"You all smell like death. You could use a shower. Is that blood? Let's get you all cleaned up. Where did you find him? In the sewer?" she said, looking at Jade.

"Not far from it. We can talk about it when we get back to Casey's. I'm afraid this is the beginning of something much bigger. What were you all discussing, it looked important?" Jade asked, nodding her head toward the cluster of people.

"You know Marta, the pregnant woman who asked you for a blessing. She has a fever, and before she fell ill, two children died. She was telling me of a tale her Nigerian mother told her about hungry spirits called Abiku. They possess the unborn child, and others like themselves hide in the aura demanding to be fed by the possessing Abiku. She insisted these spirits were the cause of the sudden illness," her mom said sadly.

Jade recalled the faces of the crying children who were trapped in the wood of the shipwreck, in the Realm of Lost Souls. Her mind ticked over, searching for logical answers even after what she had just been through. She recalled the mythological legends she had studied at school, but she had categorized them in her mind as fascinating, but fictitious stories. Great Turtle had told her about the spirit animals, the trees and nature, mostly Native American stories, which she had dismissed as she had the Greek, Egyptian, Roman, Norse, and Mexican mythological creatures. Jade long ago had decided there was no such thing. The stories were just the flavor of the era; a way for humans to explain the unexplained. Just like the Salem Witch Trials in the late seventeenth century. There had been no witches or familiars, but the rye bread had gone bad, which probably induced psychosis in the people of Salem.

But now Jade wondered how many unforeseen creatures are just out of sight. The rectangular box with her memories were in the bag with her drum and she needed to wash and open the box.

"Earth to Jade," Kevin said, snapping his fingers in front of her face.

Clouds were rolling in and it looked like it was going to storm. "Jade, are you okay?" her mom asked.

"Everything I know has been turned upside down. I have found so many forgotten memories with great-grandmother and I'm not who I thought I was. Sorry, how can we help?" Jade raised her face to catch the warmth of the sun from the parting clouds.

"The native healer has done all he can to rid Marta of the menacing spirits. He believes they are truly gone and that the soul of her unborn child has been restored, but she still believes something is wrong and she still has a fever. The herbal medicines do not seem to be working. I thought it might be psychosomatic. A group of men have gone to find more antibiotics and penicillin in case we have an outbreak, although the antibiotics she's taking don't seem to be working either."

Talking, they walked across the lawn, and Sue and Ruby came out of the lodge. Ruby was carrying a basket of food. "I'll take this to your cabin," she said.

"Sue, Ruby, this is my husband, Scott."

Her dad shook Sue's hand. "Nice to meet you. I'm famished. It's been a long time since I had any real food."

Sue was tense and had a concerned look on her face. "Does this mean you will be leaving us?"

"Not until Marta is feeling better," her mom said.

Sue's shoulders relaxed, and her frown disappeared. She was pleased Jade's mother wasn't going to leave right away.

"We'll just pop this in your cabin. Maybe your friends and family would like a rest from their hiking through the mountains."

"We're right behind you," Ellen said.

Her mom kept silent, but Jade knew there was something more on her mind. She wondered if she had seen the tattoo on her forearm and disapproved. Ruby placed the basket of food on the wooden table and took Kevin's hand. "I'll show you around the cabin if you like." There was a loft where her mother had been sleeping and two downstairs bedrooms with bunk beds. "You can rest in here," she said to Kevin and pointed to a room at her left. "This room has the nicest window. And you can rest along here," she said to Jade as she led them to the right. "It smells the nicest because it's near the bed of flowers I look after."

"That's sweet, Ruby," Kevin said. He was greeted with batting eyelashes from the ten-year-old girl.

"Come on, Ruby. Let's leave the nice folk to rest," Sue said, holding out her hand.

Jade looked at Kevin. "It looks like someone has a secret admirer." "Come sit down and have something to eat," her mother said.

"I prefer to wash before I eat. What's on your mind, Mom?"

"I was thinking, if Kevin didn't mind, after you all get some rest, he could open up a portal between two rooms to heal Marta." Her mom glanced at Kevin.

"Sure. No problem," Kevin said.

"If they find out what you can do, there might be a problem. I don't know. The community seems nice enough, but I don't want to take any risks. Your mother would never forgive me if we didn't return."

"Then, how will we do it?" Kevin said.

"I was thinking of asking the healer to make an herbal potion to put Marta to sleep and then you can create a portal and take her through. The healing properties of the portals membrane will cure her. When she wakes, she will be healed." Her mom looked at Jade and Kevin as if she was suggesting something horrible, and it pained her to say it.

"That could work," Kevin said, "but when she enters the

portal she'll wake up. We will have to rely on Marta not to tell."

"Thanks, Kevin. Get some rest, and I will organize it," her mom said.

Coming out of a quick shower, her dad dragged himself up the stairs. "I'll get something to eat later. I'm going to rest awhile and get my head together."

Jade rushed to help him, but her mom was there first.

Jade kicked off her shoes, headed for the shower, thinking about opening the box when she was alone. Then she heard a knock on the door. It was Ruby. She had brought them clean clothes.

Kevin beat her to the shower, so Jade went back to the kitchen and washed her hands and face before biting into an apple. The box and the drum sat on the table. She took her medicine pouch, notebook and backpack from Kevin's bag that he had left by the front door. Picking up her belongings, she quickly took them to her room and placed the notebook, bowie knife in its holster, drum, wand, medicine pouch, and the rectangular box, at the bottom of the bed. She sat on the bed along with all of these items and eyeballed them while eating the apple.

The window was open so she tossed the apple core into the garden and picked up the clothes Ruby had brought for Kevin. Thinking of the box and what might be inside she carried clothes to leave at the bathroom door for him. She was jolted out of her thoughts when he suddenly opened the bathroom door and steam rushed out at her. She tried not to stare, but he had a towel wrapped around his hips and he smelled so good. Her actions were clumsy as she sidestepped, to let him pass. She handed him the pile of clothing and went back to her room to collect her own clean clothes.

After her shower, Jade headed down the hall to her room and saw that Kevin was already sprawled out asleep on the bottom bunk in the room Ruby had assigned to him.

The smell of soap lingered on her skin. Jade left her tools at the bottom of her bed and crawled between the fresh sheets, but she didn't think she would sleep.

Two hours later she woke feeling refreshed, like she had slept for eight hours. She touched the drum and looked at the box. Next to the box was her wand and knife. With the tip of her finger she touched it, but felt nothing. It was just a box. She picked up the wand, shoved it in her front pocket and pulled her borrowed, oversized sweatshirt over it. Jade packed her things in her pack and tied the drum to it. She popped it at the door, ready to leave.

She went into the kitchen for some water. Outside, Kevin was awake and asking someone if they needed help. Jade stepped out to see her mom walking with Mr. Blue Eyes, who was carrying Marta in his arms. She looked very sick and frail, barely conscious. Jade pushed the door open for him to get into the cabin and showed him to the room Kevin had been resting in.

"Thanks, Mingan, we'll take it from here," Kevin said, as Mingan laid her on the lower bunk bed of Kevin's room.

"If you don't mind, I would like to watch," he said. "I'm afraid that is not possible," Jade said.

"Please help yourself to some food. We won't take long," her mom suggested, closing the door.

"Have you thought how you are going to do this, Kevin?" her mom asked.

"Yes. This room and the room Jade was in share a common wall. We will go through the wall. Jade, you'll need to help her to stand and go through the portal. Ellen, can you please wait for us to appear in the next room."

Kevin waited for her mom to leave the room and Jade put her arm underneath Marta to help her to sit on the edge of the bed. *It won't be long until the baby is born. Her stomach looked as big as Amy's just before she delivered the twins.* Marta sat on the edge of the bed, moaning. She was sweating and had that musty smell of fever and illness.

There was a familiar crackle of electricity as the particles in the air separated and created the whirlpool of liquid energy that turned into the portal. Kevin had opened the portal in the wall, then he helped Jade stand Marta up.

Marta's eyes widened and her body tensed. "Am I dead?"

"No, Marta, you're going to be healed, but please, tell no one of what you see and feel," Kevin said. "Together we are going to step into this portal; it's just a passageway of light. On the other side is Ellen, waiting for you. If there are any malicious spirits with you, or your baby, you will not be able to enter the energy of the light. If you pass through, you will be completely healed, and free of all negative energies," Kevin said. "Do you understand?"

Marta looked from one to the other, not quite sure if she should believe them. Her body was shaking, but she nodded.

"Okay then, let's go," Jade said, holding tight under Marta's arm. She was so frail, Jade thought she was going to collapse before they could get her through the portal.

"One more step, Marta," Kevin said. They moved forward.

Calm, love, and warmth washed over Jade. Emotional gasps of relief were heard from Marta, and Jade could feel the woman drawing strength. The baby was going to be a girl, an extraordinary little girl who would be courageous, loving, and kind.

Marta turned toward Jade as Kevin pulled them forward and into the room where Ellen stood against the door waiting. She ran to embrace her as soon as she was able.

"Remember, you cannot speak of what happened. This is Kevin's gift, and he wishes for it to be kept a secret for now." Jade's mom urged Marta to comply.

Ellen took Marta out to the kitchen where Mingan waited. He stood and looked at Jade and Kevin as if they had performed a miracle.

Her dad walked down the steps from the loft, unaware of what had occurred. There was something about Mr. Blue Eyes she couldn't put a finger on. She felt compelled to search his eyes and wondered if it might be an infatuation because of the beautiful color they possessed. It was hard for her to look away.

There was a knock at the door. It was Sue, returning their cleaned clothes. Her mother tried to prevent Sue from seeing into the cabin, but it was no use. She had to open the door wide, and Sue dropped the clothes on the floor in shock. "It's a miracle."

"We cannot stay. We must return to our homes," Kevin said. "My family waits for our return. But one day we will come back." He looked at Jade. "The descendant of Great Turtle will definitely be back, I'm sure of it." Jade looked at Kevin, not sure why he said she would be back. Had he seen her staring at Mingan?

Jade touched Kevin's hand with her pinky desperate to make contact with him. She didn't know what she would do if she lost him because they had gone through way too much.

"I promised his parents we would return as soon as we found Scott," her mother said.

"I understand," Sue said as her eyes scanned Marta.

"Do you want to feel the baby? She's kicking," Marta said to Sue.

Sue smiled and sat beside Marta to lay her hand on Marta's stomach and feel the baby move.

JADE AND KEVIN LEFT THE CABIN AND WALKED TO THE EDGE OF the lake. "You have a wonderful gift, K."

Looking over the lake, Jade silently let the emotions she had been bottling up over the past couple of days flow through her.

"Hey, what's wrong?" Kevin asked.

"I never truly believed I would see them together again. When mom went missing, he was a mess. And when dad went missing, mom was a mess. They fight and argue, but they love each other to bits. I was afraid I would never see them together again. I had made their lives hell. I have to redeem myself."

"I think you have enough brownie points after today to clear the slate," Kevin said.

"It was terrible, K, in the dark place. There was an ocean of tears I had to swim through. And to get to where my dad was hiding," she said, shaking her head in disbelief. "I was submerged in blood and entombed with human skulls and bones and chased by a demon. So many times I thought I was going to die. When I found him I don't even know if I was in a cave, a sewage canal or a dungeon. The only thing I was acutely aware of, was that it was a negative place. The Realm of Lost Souls is full of forgotten people with fractured souls. It was horrifying. I never want to be in a place like that again. I also thought you were dead and I'm so glad you're alright."

Kevin's hand lay by his side as he looked out at the lake, listening to Jade telling him her story, and she entwined her fingers with his. They stood watching the stillness of the water. The world had changed; she knew that, and so did Kevin.

"Let's get back to the others. Let's go home to the estate," Jade said.

"Some home-cooked food from Joe and Terry would be nice. I'm famished," Kevin said enthusiastically.

"That's a good sign."

"We can do with a few more of those," Kevin said. "By the way, can you remove the mandibles from my head and back?" Kevin said, looking anguished as he remembered they were there.

"Maybe you should leave that to your mom," Jade said.

As they began to turn away from the lake, a star appeared on the horizon. It pulsed so brightly for a few seconds, Jade thought she counted seven points. Her chest began to glow; it was like she was connected to the star. The light of the star and the light from within her were somehow communicating. When a cloud that was covering the sun moved and covered the star the light in her chest dimmed, returning it to normal.

"Wow! Jade, when did that start happening?" he said, astonished.

"While searching through the Realm of Lost Souls. I think the wand is the cause of the light." She lifted her shirt and the wand was tucked diagonally into the top of her pants. She pulled it out and gave it to Kevin to hold. Light glowed out of the wand in his hand. "Where did you get this from?"

"Chief Thundercloud. It was made for me."

"Why is it glowing? I can feel it pulsating. It's like an electrical current is waiting to explode from it."

"I don't know too much about it, but it healed my ankle. I broke it falling down a deep shaft." Jade smacked her forehead. "I could have used this to try and heal Marta."

He handed it back to Jade, and the light dimmed. "I felt energized by it. It was like a shot of coffee. That's strange," he said, seeing it dim. "Did I take its energy? Why did it shine brightly in my hand and then dim in yours?"

"You're a conductor," she said, rubbing her neck. "Let's go before it rains."

"I feel like I could sleep for a week," Kevin said, looking at his granddad's wind-up watch, which she noticed had stopped. "We'd better get back and tell Casey and Sophia what Chief Thundercloud said."

"I would like to forget everything, but I know we can't," she said. "I think in the past I chose to forget a lot. I have a lot of remembering to do. And where the hell is the fifth dimension anyway?"

"You'll remember when you're ready. Would you like to forget everything that happened on the mountain?" he said.

She pushed up the sleeves of her shirt. He was making her blush. "Hang on a minute. When did you say you got the tattoo? How long was I out for? It already looks healed."

"Just a few hours ago. The membrane of the portal has healed it of course," she said, still blushing. "Do you like it? I never thought of getting a tattoo."

"It looks great! I'm not sure your mom will agree. But I love it." He held her gaze as he said he loved it, giving her stomach butterflies.

"You smell nice too," he said. "And the tattoo goes with your hair."

She wasn't sure if that was a compliment or not. "It should come off after a while. He did it with soot," Jade said.

"No, I don't think it will. That's how they used to make ink for tats," Kevin said.

"Really?" said Jade, looking at the raven. "Well, we'd better go and get those mandibles out of your head."

Together they walked toward the cabin. They could see Jade's mom and dad idly chatting on the veranda of the main house. They bypassed the cabin because they could see her parents already had Kevin and Jade's backpacks with them.

"Ready to head back to the estate?" Kevin asked Ellen.

"Do you mind if we pop into our home first and pick up a few items?" Ellen asked.

Jade smiled as they headed off into the woods to open the portal in secret.

As Kevin created a whirlpool of energy, Jade listened to the familiar crackle of electricity. Her drum and her new friends were secure on her back. She was happy and ready to return to the others, but then Chief Thundercloud's words when he welcomed Kevin to the land of the living dead, crept back into her mind and stole her smile. She was going to have to spend time getting to know her drum and her medicine pouch. Every secret her wand reveals will have to be written in her notebook.

There was so much to think about and share with the others back at the estate—Kevin was due to open a portal for Shaun and Rachel to return from Israel tomorrow.

Jade wanted to be ready.

-The End-

GET FREE COPY OF BOOK ONE
THE EMERALD TABLET

Building a relationship with my readers is the very best thing about writing. I occasionally send newsletters with details on new releases, special offers and other bits of news relating to the Chronicles of the Supernatural and other books.

If you sign up to the mailing list I'll send you monthly free or discounted eBooks and updates of my series, The Chronicles of The Supernatural. You can sign up here and get a free copy of the first book in the series, The Emerald Tablet, if you don't have it already:

https://dl.bookfunnel.com/uab5dvpv6w

Want to keep reading, click link or type it int your URL to BUY book three, THE DEVIL'S HARVEST.

https://jmhartwriter.com/buy-now/

Enjoy this book? You can make a big difference

Reviews are the most powerful tools in my arsenal when it comes getting attention for my books. Much as I'd like to, I don't have the financial muscle of a New York publisher. I can't take out full page ads in the newspaper or put posters on the subway.

(Not yet, anyway).

But I do have something much more powerful and effective than that, and it's something that those publishers would kill to get their hands on.

A committed and loyal bunch of readers.

Honest reviews of my books help bring them to the attention of other readers.

If you've enjoyed this book I would be very grateful if you could spend just five minutes leaving a review (it can be as short as you like) on the your favorite online bookstore.

Thank you very much.

ACKNOWLEDGMENTS

I would like to thank my family and friends for their encouragements. Thank you, to the invaluable editor, Stephanie Smith, and Creativindi Cover designers, as well as JMH World Publishing's ARC team who have been a tremendous support throughout the process. No book is complete without the vital service of editors, proofreaders, and great book cover designers.

ABOUT THE AUTHOR

Now semi-retired, JM moved to a peaceful county town south of Sydney, to focus on her grandchildren and writing.
JM Hart is the author of The Chronicles of the Supernatural.
She makes her online home at:
http://jmhartwriter.com
You can also connect with JM Hart (Jeanette) on Facebook, Pinterest, and Twitter. If the mood strikes you, feel free to send her an email at author@jmhartwriter.com

www.ingramcontent.com/pod-product-compliance
Lightning Source LLC
Chambersburg PA
CBHW030424120726
47903CB00003B/802